MW01282314

PRAISE FOR **MUSCLE MAN**

"*Muscle Man* is a triumph. Jordan Castro is an outrageously gifted novelist who has given us a truly original fable of the contemporary moment. Everything in this novel is feral and brilliant, and dizzyingly funny. Castro is one of one, and this book is pure heat."
—Brandon Taylor, author of *The Late Americans*

"Jordan Castro's hilarious and astonishing new novel discovers in the insane condition of higher education surprising symptoms of the human condition."
—Michael W. Clune, author of *Pan*

"A strong, stark novel that the few men who do read must read. But women are also more than welcome, as is everyone with a heart."
—Joshua Cohen, Pulitzer Prize–winning author of *The Netanyahus*

"*Muscle Man* is a brilliant disquisition on violence, resentment, victims and victimizers, and American academia, told with the obsessive crankiness of Thomas Bernhard, acute absurdity of Donald Antrim, and a vivid linguistic hilarity all Castro's own. Made me want to feel the pump."
—Lexi Freiman, author of *The Book of Ayn*

MUSCLE MAN

ALSO BY JORDAN CASTRO

The Novelist

MUSCLE MAN

A NOVEL

Jordan Castro

CATAPULT
NEW YORK

Copyright © 2025 by Jordan Castro

First Catapult edition: 2025

ISBN: 978-1-64622-277-3

Library of Congress Control Number: 2025934363

Jacket design and illustration by Nicole Caputo
Book design by Laura Berry

Catapult
New York, NY
books.catapult.co

Printed in the United States of America

10 9 8 7 6 5 4 3 2 1

For Nicolette

ONE

I

AFTER MAKING HIS WAY, AS HE SO OFTEN DID, through the winding halls of Lawes—a bewildering labyrinth of jutting corners and walls that appeared, depending on the day, either blindingly white or damp yellow—Harold ascended the stairs, which had rubber bumpers on the edges, to protect, he thought, the students' shins but also to prevent slips, the dark brown ridges providing grip for the students' shoes, keeping them safe. The disorienting staircase—which seemed to swing as if suspended from the ceiling by thick chains, despite the fact that it was monstrously rooted in the floor—could still make students fall, he thought, or worse, although he'd never actually seen a student fall.

Harold had never actually seen a student or a group of students flung off the staircase or knocked back down the staircase landing in a heap of broken bones and bloodied faces. He had never seen the students slip and fall and pile up. Nevertheless, he noted its possibility each time he became nauseated while walking up or down the staircase, looking down so as not to make eye contact with passersby, and invariably glimpsing the brown rubber ridges. The stairs could not be made safer by any such addendum, Harold thought, because the undulating movement came from something else unseen.

The light became brighter the farther he got from his classroom.

UPSTAIRS, IN THE staff kitchen, Harold fumbled with the refrigerator door. He hadn't packed anything for lunch, and didn't expect to find anything there, but was informed in no uncertain terms by the essentially bare shelves—which contained only a half-crinkled bottle of water and some packets of condiments in the door—that he would not be able to eat before his monthly departmental meeting.

Colleges were always full of mostly empty fridges, Harold lamented, closing the refrigerator door and feeling suffocated by the walls pressing in on him, except after some event or other, when catered sandwiches remained for a few days, along with miniature bottles of water or cans of carbonated beverages. But they were never full on days when one was hungry.

The college, in short, was antithetical to strength and size, which were both qualities that Harold prized. At Shepherd College, and in Lawes most of all, the refrigerator interior remained a humming, uninviting white. The college was teeming with people whose diets more closely resembled snakes' than people's, not eating all day and then binge-eating later, on microwaved or delivered food, in front of piles of papers, often with the television on, mindlessly ingesting, glassy-eyed.

Harold was disgusted when any of his colleagues mentioned food: "I microwave raw chicken to thaw it all the time!"; "I told myself I wouldn't eat the whole sleeve of Oreos, but what could I do—you know how I get when I read *Jane Eyre*."

There was no need for a refrigerator, Harold thought, or even a kitchen—kitchen*ette*—at this or any other college.

Light crisscrossed unpredictably as Harold exited the kitchenette; the sun shot in through the thick windows, then dispersed across the speckled crowd; his eyes widened, then became small. There was no sun in the classroom he'd been assigned this semester, in the basement, so he hadn't seen light for around an hour and a half, with the exception of the fluorescent light, which was indistinguishable, at least to his abnormally small and close-set eyes, from darkness.

The octagonal opening outside the kitchenette contained a confused swarm of students, teachers, and administrators, each walking purposefully toward one of the many halls that unfurled out from the center like tentacles. Harold walked straight, then turned slightly right.

Casey? he thought. His heart fluttered. Casey was

Harold's most esteemed colleague, and his only friend in the department. Casey's first book, which Harold envied, was about the history of the way thought was rendered in the novel, and his second was about the relationship between the body and literature—calling for what Casey termed "embodied literature"—which spanned nearly every discipline, synthesized many disparate ideas creatively, and was written in a style that laypeople could actually understand. Casey exuded a mastery of his subject and had an irresistible social pull. Those in his orbit were immediately put at ease. His towering intellect wasn't icy; rather, it lulled one into a not-quite-submission, in which one felt free but also warm, tinged with trusting adoration. Harold was particularly grateful to Casey, because Casey had, among other things, brought Harold to the gym for the first time.

So Harold was happy to run into Casey. But when the man in the hall turned, his ill-proportioned face cried out the sad fact of his nonidentity: the way his ears folded over at the top, and his nose was turned up like a pug's—this was not Casey. Casey would not be caught dead in these halls at this time, Harold reconsidered, because, unlike Harold, he would never go to a meeting twenty minutes early.

Harold's creaky head had been hurting all morning, which he attributed to hunger, but as he walked toward the meeting room, his headache gradually dissipated, despite the fact that he still hadn't eaten, having decided that he would intentionally continue what he had quickly begun to think of as his "fast"—a mental trick he used to make his hunger feel productive. It was early March, still cold, but Harold had been meaning to stop bulking, so he could slim back down for warmer weather anyway: Harold was currently 195 pounds, abs still somewhat visible, at least when he sucked in and flexed, up from 173 at the beginning of the fall semester, when he was shredded, around 7 or 8 percent body fat.

Now Harold was likely around 17 percent. His cheeks were puffy and full of water and they jiggled when he moved too quickly. In pictures, he looked like a different kind of person than he was: one who laughed loudly, in a good-natured way; who delighted in simple things and handled problems graciously; a man who didn't take himself too seriously—a "jolly" man.

In the hall, Harold imagined his body eating away at the layer of fat between his muscle and skin; he could feel it, the subtle gurgle and sear, which he imagined he could hear—then actually began to hear—as the sound of his fat being burned in his cheeks dimly hummed in the seat of his skull.

He waded through the throbbing hall.

THE MAHOGANY TABLE IN THE CENTER OF THE meeting room was engraved with horses, swords, shields, and human heads. Beneath the table, at the center of the X-stretcher beams, was a carved, fire-like ornament. From a distance, it appeared sentient.

Like all the furniture at Shepherd, the table—and its heavy, creaking chairs, which seemed to sigh or shudder as he sat—had initially disturbed Harold. But over time he had developed a method for making it all feel harmonious: when he imagined himself alone with the table, or imagined the table on its own, out of context, the knotted wood transfigured itself into something resembling not a fire but a bouquet.

It wasn't unless everything was taken together, in its absolute totality, that the furniture, along with the walls and the old paintings of old men, nearly suffocated him. Even the couches in the lounge seemed to envelop their inhabitants a little too eagerly—it was not uncommon to find students asleep on them.

The construction of the college had been disjointed over time. The architect initially tasked with designing Shepherd College practiced a method called "organic architecture," which emphasized harmony between his human structures and the natural environment; the buildings were meant to integrate with their surroundings, smooth and simple, utilizing light and open space, so that students could think clearly.

However, as enrollment went up over decades, the campus needed more buildings, and the new architect they hired to design these buildings—which included Lawes—had different, more "modern" ideas about education.

In a short, out-of-print book outlining his philosophy, the architect responsible for Lawes, an American phenomenologist who wrote under the pen name R. K. Mort, argued that "real education" could take place only in an "abnormal, dizzying" setting: the goal of education, he wrote, was to create people who were *unlike* other people, and, since buildings both influenced and reflected their inhabitants, he sought to design everything just a little bit off—a slightly rounded corner, a ceiling that slanted almost imperceptibly. He did not want the building to be straightforwardly jarring, like a fun house or an amusement park, but rather subtly unsettling, so that those studying would "teeter on the edge of the visible and invisible worlds, always subconsciously aware that things are not quite as they seem." This, for him, was the impetus of all knowledge: the desire to see *through* things, because the surface was not meaningful—the surface was where meaning died. R. K. Mort wanted the building to "infect," he wrote, even "haunt," those inside it, so that the work they did might not so easily conform to the world around them but remain "set apart," either "above, or below, it doesn't matter, the mere face of things." Mort believed in the power of place; he did not believe in perfect angles or "comforting lies"; he detested rote memorization, which he saw already emerging in his time, so he created what he thought of as a building that was "faithful to the living, breathing dissonance" of life.

Knowledge itself was inorganic, he wrote, and served only the purpose of "directing" humanity's "attack on the environment."

Then there was the furniture. The furniture in Lawes was not the original furniture but had been planted by a committee two generations after Mort's death. Some of the committee members had made a PowerPoint, going over the fundamentals of Mort's ideas, which had survived only in their simplest form, and, given budgetary concerns—in addition to concerns about some of his more "eccentric" ideas about genetics—the committee decided not to follow the dead architect's lead, but rather to "give the students a broader, more inclusive historical sense" by sampling many different kinds of furniture from many different time periods and many different parts of the world.

However, almost all the furniture was created by a single company.

As opposed to Mort's goal of disorienting and disrupting students, this committee sought "clarity" and even "consolation," in addition to their primarily sociological concerns.

The result was total incoherence. Now the furniture was over ten years old and appeared haphazard and half-displaced, an old-new simulacrum of something even older. The furniture looked to Harold like a representation of furniture. The tabletop where Harold sat was vaguely waxy, perhaps recently polished, though the deep brown had accrued many nicks and skids over time, as if a child had taken a butter knife to it. At the four corners of the table were pillars—Greek Ionic columns—at the top of which the wood curled down like ribbons. They reminded Harold of upside-down books, and when he sat at the corner—his favorite place to sit—he often fondled what he thought of as the table's "pages."

This time, alone, with eighteen minutes until the meeting, Harold sat with his back to the heavy doors, where a small wooden head jutted out over the awning, with a plaque that read, "The End of our Foundation is the knowledge of Causes, and secret motions of things; and the enlarging of the bounds of Human Empire, to the effecting of all things possible. —Francis Bacon, *New Atlantis*."

Harold read the plaque and reprimanded himself again for not having packed a lunch. He didn't want to starve his muscles. He wanted to eat something high in protein with fast-digesting carbs: chicken and rice, steak and potatoes. He yearned to grind animal flesh between his teeth, to feel the dead muscle resist, then give, against his jaw.

Harold tapped the table with his palms—he hated meetings. Harold hated meetings, but he hated waiting for meetings even more, because he hated having free time. So-called free time was never really free, Harold had considered over his teaching career—five years as a lecturer, then five as an associate professor—which seemed to curse him with an unusual amount of it: there was no such thing as "free time," and it was during so-called free time when one was most enslaved, acting only in the most abject ways, blindly following this or that whim, pulled by amorphous and undifferentiated forces, self-scattering.

The "free" in "free time" was of that strange phraseology that denoted the exact opposite of what it purported to mean: one had free time, and without giving it a second thought, he sat down in front of his television, or laptop, or phone, and navigated thoughtlessly to something that might take his mind off his condition, and even if he was not in front of a screen but for some reason passing time in the physical world, his brain was still filled with fragmented, combative distractions, swirling endlessly until they finally got directed toward something concrete and specific. Without purpose, time spread out around him and engulfed him. The only thing more powerful than time was an orienting vision, or a goal.

Harold's only goal was to get out of this meeting as quickly as possible, then get to the gym. This was a bad goal. The meeting hadn't even started yet, and its duration would be out of his control. Harold had time, or rather time had him—Harold was sitting at the table *with time*—and, since he didn't have a meal or protein shake, he was directionless and undefined. Lunch could have empowered him to use these twenty minutes productively: the food would have given him something to do in the present, then more energy to use later in the gym, which would lead to the accrual of more muscle mass. Like time, action spread out into the future. Action was a form of time.

Harold gripped the knobs on the chair's arms. Why hadn't he packed a lunch? The college always seemed to intentionally schedule classes and meetings too close together or too far apart, leaving awkward amounts of time in between, such that everyone in Lawes was always either sprinting or shuffling, bumping into and around each other, too hurried or too slow, clunking up against each other, then dispersing. Harold felt sick. He hated his job.

The pattern of the students in the hall in between classes mirrored the layout of the building, with its narrow corridors converging disconcertingly upon each other, spitting students out into a dim back corner or a wide-open common area with too few places to sit, every bench spread awkwardly across the exposed floor, like shards of a shattered mirror.

The swarming mass of students Harold had encountered in the hall appeared as fragments of something large and singular and living, or like maggots wriggling beneath an overturned rock.

At least I don't have to teach anymore today, Harold thought, sinking in his chair.

This comforted him momentarily, but the feeling of his basement classroom still stuck with him like a curse.

Ever since Harold's first encounter with Lawes' convoluted enclosures, when he came for a campus visit and got lost in the halls for thirty minutes—scurrying, desperately trying to follow the numbers on doors, which in many cases did not move sequentially but jumped around without reason—Harold couldn't shake the feeling that he would never escape.

III

AS HE SAT ALONE IN THE MEETING ROOM, Harold's thoughts were constantly interrupted by students buzzing past, such that he could neither finish a thought nor clear his mind. Since he had nothing to eat, he figured he might as well try to do some thinking, perhaps to find a new connection between some old ideas that he could turn into a paper, or to strike upon something totally new, as he had dreamed of doing now for many years, but the mass of students in the hall prevented him. So he took out his phone and navigated to his workout app.

Harold tapped the "Calendar" button and looked at his plan for the day. He was in the second month of a three-month hypertrophy program. Today was chest and triceps. Harold scanned the screen, but his eyes creased as he imagined how he would likely feel weaker than usual, due to hunger. He navigated out of the app and forcefully banished the thought from his mind: he would, he resolved, simply *get in the zone* and *lift heavy*.

It wouldn't be hard, Harold thought, sitting at what he had begun to think of semi-ironically as "the ancient table," fondling one of its ridges, to access the proper mindset in the gym: the weight always felt lighter after departmental meetings. Departmental meetings, Harold had once told Casey, were "mindset invigorators," instilling a special kind of passion in him. Usually, when Harold lifted, he tried to focus on being present with the weight; he tried to forget everything, as best he could, and think single-mindedly about his muscles. After meetings, however, Harold harnessed a different kind of power. Harold's colleagues' voices would linger in him long after they'd parted, leaking across time into his head and taking on a life of their own, such that he would occasionally imagine himself as one or another of them, saying the exact things they'd said but in a slightly different tone, almost as if he wanted to become them, or was remembering a distant desire to become them, as he pressed a barbell up toward the ceiling or squatted down and then stood up again. Harold did not derive any obvious pleasure from this bizarre mental exercise, which had emerged only semiconsciously. One day he simply noticed he was doing it, but, since he didn't tell anyone about it, harboring and compartmentalizing it like a secret, he more or less forgot about it when he wasn't in the gym.

Harold detested his colleagues, but at times he imagined wearing their clothes, or their skin. When he was interacting with people at the gym, exchanging pleasantries and so on, he would imagine that they were actually interacting with David or Vance or even Dolly instead of him. These mystical visions, which filled him with a subtle sense of justice, or self-actualization, seemed to possess him: he would simply "be" Vance with his rosy cheeks, or Dolly in a sundress, and he only ever realized that he'd been one of them afterward, once the interaction was over and he was walking toward the weights alone, as some glitchy, unsatisfactory version of himself.

Harold had also been getting emails, vaguely referencing some new "investigations." He didn't read them in full, but he could tell—based on the vague shapes of the letters and a general impression of the tone—that they were extensions of the university's efforts to keep students and faculty abreast of crime. Any time a crime was committed on campus, the campus police sent out "alerts," reporting certain details of the crime: what had taken place and where, whether or not the area was "clear." There had been a wave of strange occurrences: random violent outbursts, thefts, students masturbating in daylight on the benches outside. One American history professor, who was only forty-five, had simply fallen over dead in the middle of the hall. Students weren't coming to classes or completing assignments. They weren't even emailing to ask if they could make anything up. When they did email, usually asking for a better grade, the emails contained no punctuation and numerous typos; an apathetic contempt emanated from every demand. There were also pranks: a portable electric stove, boiling a giant pot of water and plant matter in the middle of the hall; period blood smeared across the wall of a classroom, perhaps attempting to spell FREEDOM but instead spelling only FREEDO.

The emails didn't call these actions "crimes." They didn't even call it a "crime" when someone was found stabbed multiple times, bleeding out on a street near one of the off-campus buildings. Rather, these "alerts" were "opportunities to get inspired to consider new ways of thinking about how we might better relate to and understand one another." What material circumstances might compel someone, for example, to follow a woman down the street shrieking obscenities at her? What might have been the systemic cause of the student's getting stabbed twenty-three times in the back? And how might better scholarship, or better pedagogy, prevent it?

These new emails were sent from a different department than the usual notifications—instead of SHPRDALERT@shepherd.edu, the emails came from ALERT_TO_INSPIRE@shepherd.edu. Harold's inbox was often spammed with Shepherd-related announcements. He had developed a habit of selecting new emails quickly, then deleting them unopened, to rid his inbox of the clutter, but a morbid curiosity always caused him to click the "alert to inspire" emails.

Sitting at the ancient table, Harold tried to focus

on the stores of fat his body was burning, but he was distracted by the sounds of howling students. Voices seemed to scream out from the floor, mixing with fragments of what would have been Harold's thoughts. He sucked in his cheeks and his stomach and squinted.

Harold imagined all of his colleagues standing around him as he sat, anxiously observing him, as if he were a caged monkey, wondering what he might do next. I am free, Harold thought as he imagined standing up—no, jumping up—and dancing a jig, waving his arms above his head, flinging the lower portion of his legs by hinging and extending each knee violently. Harold could do anything. Harold was *one*, and his colleagues were *all*. It wasn't just that Harold was different from Vance or Dolly or John but that they were all the same. Harold could bend them to his will, he thought, by doing anything that went against their expectations. Harold usually said "Vance" while talking to Vance, and "Dolly" while talking to Dolly, but he could, he thought twitchily, just as easily say "Vance" when talking to Dolly, or "Dolly" when talking to Vance, and no one would notice. In fact, Harold had, on occasion, yelled "Vance" in order to get Dolly's attention or "Dolly" to get Vance's attention, and in every single instance they had turned around. In conversations with other colleagues, Harold would sometimes say "Vance" to mean Dolly, or "Dolly" to mean Vance, and his colleagues' eyes would not so much as blink.

I will have them right where I want them, Harold thought . . . They will all talk about my sudden jig. Or should I stand up and pretend to confess to some horrible crime?

Harold smiled maniacally and squirmed in his chair. This was going to be a great meeting, he resolved. The *jig meeting*. He suddenly recalled how, at the last meeting, he'd averted his eyes when Vance looked at him for longer than Harold expected. Vance was a Chaucer scholar; he taught Old English and Middle English poetry. He was in his late fifties and wore large, round glasses; his gray hair puffed out the sides of a baseball cap that covered his bald spot. His enormous rectangular chin swallowed his neck, and his legs seemed to sprout directly out of his chest.

What was Vance's problem? Harold thought again, as he had then. This time, Harold resolved, I will hold Vance's eyes for as long as he wishes. I will hold them until my own eyes dry up and fall out of my sockets, if need be. I will hold Vance's eyes and I will not let them go no matter what, and I will win!

Suddenly thirsty, Harold got up and swung the heavy wooden door out into the cacophony of voices in the hall. It was going to be a fine day. He was going to hold Vance's eyes and jump up and dance a jig and it was going to be a fine day. But as soon as Harold entered the hall, his resolve disappeared. He shrunk. A high-pitched ringing filled his ears.

It isn't nothing, Harold thought, that my ears feel incredibly hot, and it's not nothing that the ringing seems to be coming from both inside and outside of my hot ears . . .

Harold clamped his hands over his ears and muscled his eyelids wide.

The faces in the hall appeared either too long and stretched or scrunched up and small, emitting noises but no words, or words Harold could not understand. Limbs stretched over everything like unspooled yarn, mouths and walls making the same sad sound, a kind of scream-yawn, obliteration song—bodies marching, leaderless army—trampling Harold, crushing him into a sticky, dehydrated dust.

Harold saw something glint in the outside pocket of a student's black backpack. His heart flitted with a mix of fear and joy.

Why would a student have something like that here? Especially for someone like me to see so clearly? His heart began to beat as he considered, not forming thoughts so much as experiencing some other sensation, whether or not he should confirm what he had seen, and before Harold could process what was happening, his legs had taken him farther away from the meeting room and down the hall after the student.

Harold kept his distance, shifting his weight between his two feet unevenly but trying to step steadily, so as not to create a conspicuously uneven sound, and snaking in and out of view, so if the student, hearing Harold's off-beat gait, turned around to fix his purposes on him, he might be hidden behind another student, or an open door. But after just a few moments in the disorienting corridors of Lawes, Harold had trouble differentiating among the people around him:

clothes and backs of heads appeared identical; the faces looked the same as backs of heads. And so, instead of the student, Harold focused on trying to spot the glinting object.

I am a snoop, and I have always been a snoop, Harold thought. For as long as I can remember I have always been a snoop. Harold rehearsed this to himself, as if preparing for an argument, as he zigzagged through the Lawes halls in pursuit of the student.

I have always been a snoop, Harold thought, although that's no fault of my own. It's my temperament. It's useful. What would the world be like, he thought, if no one was ever *curious*; if no one ever went around looking into things and trying to get to the bottom of them? What would the world be like if no one *cared*?

Harold continued down the hall, scanning the muted hues for something bright. The fluorescent light infected every surface with a dull, flattening glare. Harold was functionally blind. Normal objects appeared menacingly obscure, as in a dark wood.

Harold began to doubt his initial observation. He had often said that the college was "murderous"—but not this kind of murderous. Sure, there had been one stabbing. Or rather, two. There was Jonathan Larmey, a couple of years ago, then another more recently— which had been so similar to the Larmey stabbing that some faculty had taken to calling it a "copycat killing"—but it was unthinkable for there to be multiple in the same year. Was it possible he had imagined what he saw? Had the glinting object been in his mind?

No—he had seen what he had seen. And if something were to happen . . .

I could go report it, he thought, just to be safe.

But what would he even say?

Hey, I saw a glinting . . . No, *I . . . I'd like to report a . . .* No.

There was no student, he attempted to convince himself. There was nothing sharp and bright. Harold had been mistaken. He had gotten carried away. And if he was not mistaken, he thought, he could just pretend he hadn't seen anything. The last thing anyone needed was more draconian oversight, more meetings, more mandatory this and that. One or two incidents did not always require structural change. *But what if this student was looking for me?* He almost choked as he inhaled.

Harold imagined lifting the student up by the collar, the bright object falling to the floor. He was a hero. He imagined being stabbed in front of everyone, the knife penetrating his ribs, and his organs, repeatedly, hundreds of times, the student stabbing him even after he'd died . . .

Just then, Harold saw a student place a black backpack on the ground. A crowd of art students, Harold recognized from their wide pants, walked past, then stopped to chat with the student who had put his backpack down. Without giving it any thought, but feeling compelled by a strange notion of "justice," Harold pressed into the small crowd and, apologizing while waving his left hand over his head, took the backpack in his right, holding it down at his side, then pulled it up around and squeezed it to his chest.

So what, Harold thought, half-consciously. I have always been a curious man. I have always wanted to save the college from itself. He clutched the bag and walked as fast as he could—driving through the balls of his feet and squeezing his glutes to generate maximal power—until he'd zigzagged around a couple of corners, then hurried back toward the meeting room.

What did it really amount to? he thought. Anyone with half a brain would do just as I have done. But no one at Shepherd had even half a brain. That was the problem. The college was teeming with a kind of less-than-half-brainedness, an anti-curiosity; no one went out in search of anything with stakes; no one had skin in the game.

Harold had skin and a brain. And he had muscles. Harold blinked and walked quickly. Was this the backpack he had seen before? This wasn't the first time Harold had taken something from a student. But everybody had their excesses. Especially those who aspired to something better than the drudgery of mediocrity. Every genius or near-genius had his excesses. A small thing here or there was a small price to pay.

Panting and standing now against a wall to catch his breath, Harold thought about various great men in history. Who among them didn't have some insoluble problem? How could one assert with absolute certainty that those problems weren't positively correlated with their greatness? Pull one thread and the whole of greatness might unravel into a pile. Harold could overlook a lot for greatness. It was rare—and one shouldn't meddle too much when it was present, in another, or in oneself.

Harold stood completely still. He took his phone out, clammy handed, clutching the black bag to his chest.

IV

BACK IN THE MEETING ROOM, HAROLD OPENED
Instagram. He tried not to think about the backpack.
Although he didn't really have to try—once he'd
opened Instagram, he just didn't think about it. He
merely sat back down, heart beating a little faster than
usual, placed the backpack at his feet, and took his
phone out of his pocket.

Harold's head felt hazy, like he was at a distance
from himself.

When his eyes focused on his phone, his brain
seemed to shoot to the front of his forehead, then thud
against the bone, causing his lips to curl—he loved the
weightlifting meme accounts. When a meme account
was truly a meme account, and not merely a meme
disseminator, its mimetic power spread, such that it
spawned many similar accounts, and the comments

beneath each post were written in the same style as the meme. In short, a true meme account would exist at the center of an orbit of imitators, and would embrace them, creating an idiosyncratic world of endlessly proliferating in-jokes, with its own lexicon and style. Harold's Instagram feed consisted mostly of these memes now, especially since he'd unfollowed many of the accounts he used to follow: university programs, academics, and writers, who rarely posted and who, when they did post, only posted pictures of books or excerpts of books, scenery, cookies and pastries.

The American universities had died, but they had also gone on living, and nowhere was their dead-aliveness, their *zombification*, more apparent than online, where schools posted about events—always sparsely attended, garnering measly double-digit "likes," with words like "exciting," "excited," "please join," and "announce"—and other dull bulletins having to do with new hires, contests, or publications.

Academics themselves often had private accounts. Harold initially assumed that this was because they were posting things that would get them into trouble if they were public, or personal things that were disharmonious with their image as intellectuals; but after he followed a number of them, eagerly anticipating access to their true selves, he realized that their accounts were private not out of prudence but out of meekness: pictures of piles of books (their "stacks"), piles of papers with captions cheekily bemoaning their course load, maybe a glass of wine or a sandwich. If the zombification of colleges was apparent in their public-facing profiles online, the zombification of individual academics was apparent in their private profiles, which were even more unsettling, as they betrayed a soullessness more befitting a bug than a person. Their pages were occasionally littered with infographics, as well as various "calls to action," pertaining to whatever "cause" had been hastily circulating among them most recently. These posts would then appear like fossils, crystallized on their grid, eerily out of sync with the rest of their posts, and appearing out-of-date just a day or two after the mimetic frenzy that had led to the post ended. But the meme accounts, often irreverent and surprising, brought Harold joy.

Harold glanced down at the backpack, then returned to his phone.

The first post was a video of a bodybuilder doing hanging leg raises—an ab exercise where one hangs from a pull-up bar and lifts their legs straight out in front of them—with the text THE DOCTOR SAID I HAVE A DISABILITY at the top of the video, and DIS ABILITY TO ANALYZE, DECONSTRUCT, IMPROVE AND DOMINATE . . . YES I AM AN INTJ LIFTER at the bottom. A rap song played over the video. Harold clicked the side button on his phone three times quickly, to turn the volume down, in case anyone were to walk into the room.

Harold scrolled quickly past an image of a painting, then a picture of a tree.

The next meme was a picture of Mel Keyes, a bodybuilder who had become a kind of model for Harold, despite his having been dead for fifteen years. Harold had spent countless hours reading Mel's books and articles, and watching interviews with him online. Harold felt like he knew Mel even better than Casey, whom he considered his best friend, even though Casey had been the one to tell Harold about Mel.

In the meme, Mel was shirtless with his arms crossed; a woman was wrapped around his arm, looking lovingly up at him while he looked straight ahead. Everything was gold tinged. There was a close-up of the Sistine Chapel in the background, God's finger reaching out to Adam's but not quite making contact, due to Adam's slightly bent finger. Overlaid on the image, in red-outlined white text: IT'S EASY KID / JUST FOLLOW ME.

Harold scrolled and saw an advertisement for his own college, saying "Learn more about our history," with a link to the Shepherd College website.

Fffff... he thought. The algorithm had gotten so effective that it was advertising Harold's own place of employment back to him. What kind of imbecile would want to click something like this?

Harold clicked, to see what his brilliant employers were up to.

Shepherd College opened in 1859 as the town of Bly's first agriculture school, purchased from a slaveholding farmer, and built on ancestral Piscataway land, it read, in large, bold, italicized font. The link had taken Harold to the "History and Mission" section of the college's website. This must have been added recently, Harold thought—he had never seen it mentioned anywhere publicly before.

Harold involuntarily looked down at the back-pack. He snapped his neck toward his phone and tried to focus on the screen.

Years ago, while Harold was waiting to meet the dean on his initial campus visit, one of the administrative assistants, sitting at her desk in the waiting room, told Harold this same information. They had been talking a little about the college when she curled her fingers and started rubbing the tips of them against her palms in a fit of excitement.

"Nearby," she said, smiling, "over at Harbor Bay—which is a great place for kayaking or hiking, if you're into that sort of thing—there are over a hundred ship-wrecks rotting underwater." This was when Harold first noticed her eyes. They didn't move. But Harold expected them to move, so in accordance with his expectation he imagined that they twitched, or shifted, in his periphery, and he was unsettled to notice that, when he looked at them directly to confirm that they had moved, they were in fact completely still, like glass.

"There used to be this thing in the 1800s called 'shanghaiing,'" she'd said, "I guess some racist reference to China. These companies would set up board-inghouses along the water, to attract drunks and drug addicts and gamblers, right? But then the boarding-house people—what do you call them? residents?—would wake up, having been drugged, and learn that they had signed a contract basically making them slaves for these shipping companies, and they'd have to be sailors forever." As the woman spoke, Harold was seized by the instinct to flee. He glanced at the dean's office door. Despite her motionless eyes, the secretary seemed to notice that Harold was growing impatient, and instead of easing up and accommodating his palpable discomfort, her tone became more forceful.

"The boats were from World War I," she continued. "They say the shipwreck was because of a curse. Something to do with the Piscataway tribe." She said it slowly, piscuh-*tah*-way, as if demonstrating how to properly pronounce the word, though in fact it was a mispronunciation. She paused. "I don't really believe in all of that, but it does kind of feel like there are ghosts here." Her eyes seemed to shift for a fraction of a second. "It's probably just the way everything *looks*, though. I'm not used to all this." The secretary tilted her head, but there was no way to know what she was referring to. Around them, there were chairs and a coffee table, a framed poster of the cover of *To Kill a Mockingbird*. Harold thought that the secretary might have been gesturing toward something invisible. She laughed. Her eyes softened and met Harold's and she gave him a knowing nod.

The history reminded Harold of the beginning of one of the Gothic novels he taught in class: the backdrop of a haunted present, the sins of past generations traversing time and space to meet him where he sat.

None of us are innocent, Harold thought, quoting himself from class earlier that week, when he was describing what many Gothic novels seemed to teach. But neither are we guilty in the sense of being uniquely responsible. We are, Harold thought, as if teaching—he always thought more cogently while imagining himself teaching—haunted; caught in a web of relations that stretch backward in time. Responsibility is spread around such that it belongs to all of us, fairly or not, he thought. And we can't extricate ourselves from it. There is a force that stretches back to the foundation of the world . . . something once hidden, now revealed . . .

That fateful day on campus, Harold had eventually begun to feel a combination of gratitude for his new job but also piercing fear. From the moment he arrived on the campus, with its colonial columns and brick, its interiors of immense wood and stone; its history of a kind of rise, then decline—a history that all American colleges shared—Harold felt that the campus was concealing something frightfully duplicitous. And that this duplicity was personified in the administrative assistant with glass eyes.

This sense of some dark underbelly came as a shock to Harold. He had begun his career full of hope. He had been excited to break free from the confines of society, and to enter into communion with the great thinkers of history. Academia promised a glimmering future, one in which worldly concerns were secondary to the pursuit of what he then viewed as higher ambitions. Harold would be a kind of priest, he thought, studying and transmitting what he'd learned to those whom he would then mold in his image. And, like a priest, Harold would instruct his students in the most important aspects of life: literature, culture, philosophy. Harold had always loved reading and writing—this was all he ever loved—and to be able to read and write for a living felt unimaginably lucky. Harold had come from a working-class family, who had never understood his obsession with books; even his friends thought him strange for his passion, which at times had made him awkward and asocial.

Harold had always known he had a great mind, which he'd tried to explain to his friends growing up, when they would taunt him and call him "gay." He tried to put it in a way they'd understand. "With a book," Harold told his best friend, "you can communicate with the smartest people, without being oppressed by any kind of obligation to them. You can just put them down and pick them up. Imagine that power: being able to pick up and put down the greatest thinkers in history. Living people swarm you and try to suck you like mosquitos. They *want* and *ask* and *smell*. With books it's a whole different thing."

Harold's friends still didn't care. "It's even better than that," he continued to push, "because you can actually take dead people's brains and get them into your head." He had been waiting to pull this out as a last resort. His friends looked at him uneasily. "When you read, you actually get to replace your own head with another person's head."

But Harold's immediate impression of Lawes was one of a strange kind of imprisonment, not the freedom he had found in books. Of course, he didn't let himself articulate this; he didn't think about it at all; nevertheless, it caused a strange feeling to settle into him. Perhaps it was just the uneasiness of freedom,

Harold thought, cautiously—or was he surrounded by something legitimately sinister?

The natural landscape of Shepherd College was picturesque, marred only by the campus's aesthetic inconsistencies. The hodgepodge of materials and styles gave Harold a claustrophobic feeling, like he was scrolling on his phone; the buildings, like the furniture, looked like pictures, or images on a screen, flatly representing something that only might have once been real.

But other than this, Harold could not locate his fear in anything rational. There were material explanations for everything, and Harold, being a product of some of the best minds in academia, believed them. The relative *otherness* of the architecture at Shepherd, and in particular Lawes—in addition to his meeting various new people for the first time—likely caused his amygdala to flood the body with adrenaline and cortisol. The amygdala signaled his hypothalamus, which signaled his pituitary gland; his pituitary gland sent ACTH hormone into the blood; the adrenal gland released epinephrine, as his body responded to the new stimulus as a potential threat. So, shaking his head at the sensation that he was inhabiting something cosmically hostile, he reminded himself that he was just having a natural, temporary physiological response.

But there were other oddities too, like the way the wind swept through the center of campus, causing everything but the birch branches to move; or how the ceilings in the administration offices were so low that tall students were able to write on them—Harold

looked up once and saw HELLPP MEEE and IS-
LAM IS RIGHT ABOUT WOMEN scratched into
the paint. There were other things too, which caused
Harold to retain the strange conviction that Shepherd College, which prided itself on its progressive
pedagogies and spirit of scientific inquiry, which
claimed to *teach* and *foster* and *create*, was ultimately
doing no such thing.

When Harold left campus after that first visit, he
forgot about the administrative assistant, and he hadn't
seen or thought about her again until now, looking at
the Shepherd website, waiting for his meeting to start.
When he'd returned to the lobby after meeting with
the dean, she wasn't there. Then, as now, this information about the college's past was presented to him out
of nowhere, which made Harold suspicious.

Often, we tell half-truths in order to conceal a full
truth, opting for a false kind of confession that serves
only to perpetuate a greater lie. We conceal something
more dreadful by exposing something less dreadful,
but still dreadful, so the audience we are half confid-
ing in is deceived by our performance of vulnerability.
Even though the college was making "progress"—
incorporating some ugly aspects of its past into the
present—something still felt unexcavated, as if the
college had only pretended to present something dead
and dug up from its depths, when in reality it was pre-
senting something scarily still-alive.

Harold tapped the screen, out of the Shepherd
College website, and landed back on his Instagram
feed. He scrolled down to the next meme: a screenshot

of a tweet from *Cosmopolitan* magazine with the text "I went through my boyfriend's phone and saw things I wasn't prepared for" and a link to an article, with an image beneath it: three bodybuilders in Speedos holding hands, smiling victoriously.

V

HAROLD PICKED UP THE BACKPACK AND SAT it on his lap like a child.

The zipper pulls were made of dense, dark metal, with cross-shaped holes in the center. The bag was monochromatic: its black compartments and black zippers and black neoprene fabric made it look like a hole. Even the straps were black.

Harold tugged at the zipper of the largest compartment.

He extended his hand into the black hole cautiously, as if he were touching a woman for the first time, a strange and thrilling kind of intimacy. The physical sensation of the objects against his skin came before he could visualize them: smooth, thin plastic . . . knot . . . —cords, charger?—rough, flat surface, small crinkly square—library book—spiral notebook spine—more crinkling—wrappers?—some fabric—nothing sharp.

Harold's finger flicked the edge of something tubular and hollow. At first, he thought it could be a silencer on a gun, but as he traced his finger along its outer edge he discerned that it was not made of steel. It was a giant... tube? The cardboard core of a paper towel roll? Harold wrapped his fingers around the object. He pulled it out.

It was a poster, rolled up in a rubber band. Someone might walk in at any moment, Harold remembered, as he hurriedly pushed the rubber band off.

I could just show them the poster, he thought, weakly, if someone comes in. But then how will I explain it?

I won't explain it, Harold resolved. I won't explain myself. I am above these cretinous, nosy, explanation-obsessed bugs, who might at any moment clumsily flutter into the room, toward me, like moths to light.

Harold unfurled the large, laminated paper. The font at the top resembled lightning, each letter zigged and zagged sharply: *FAITH GROUP FOR MARGINALIZED IDENTITIES*. There was a clip-art outline of the Star of David, an Islamic star and crescent, and other symbols Harold didn't recognize; there was a cartoon menorah that looked like Lumière from *Beauty and the Beast*, with bulging eyes, rosy cheeks, and a speech bubble near its mouth that said "Shalom!" Beneath that were other greetings, sprinkled at different angles: "Assalamualaikum," "Namaste," "Yo!"

Marginalized identities... Like "lifter"? Harold

thought, adopting the ironic tone of the memes he'd just been looking at. Harold tried to lean back in the stiff chair, but instead of reclining like he wanted—lengthening his hip flexors and stretching—he stayed cramped and bent.

Harold often encountered the phrase "marginalized people"—events or products were often "for marginalized people" or "in solidarity with members of marginalized communities"—but "marginalized identities" felt wrong somehow, perhaps because "identities" were not alive. A freshman must have made the poster, Harold thought. Whoever made it would have a better grasp on their new language soon enough.

Lawes had its own language, which billowed and unfurled and swallowed the students.

Harold stood up all at once. He dropped the poster and pushed it beneath the table with his foot, pressing down with too much force at first, then letting up a bit so that it slid, forcing it and crinkling it until only a corner was visible from where he sat.

The poster curled up into the roping wood, and for a moment it appeared to be on fire. Harold needed to leave. He needed to do *something*. The backpack did not have many identifying features besides the cross zippers, which one could only see from up close; perhaps he could carry it around the halls, he thought, carry it on his back, acting natural—and this little thrill perked him up a bit. Why would anyone suspect anything? It was normal to wear a backpack at college. Harold gripped the zipper, pressing his finger into the cross hole until it imprinted on his thumb, then he zipped the bag shut. He stood up, slung the backpack over his shoulder, and scurried to the door.

If someone stopped and questioned him, he could always just say he'd found it, and was planning on returning it after his meeting . . .

Fffff, he thought, as he pushed open the door and glanced out into the pulsing hall. Dolly's brown bob bounced in the distance. He froze. He pulled the door closed again and stood shivering in the meeting room.

Why did I so stupidly choose to wait here? he accused himself. If anyone came early—and surely someone would come early; *Dolly* was coming early—he'd be forced to explain the bag.

If my colleagues know anything about me, he thought, if they have been observant of me in the least—really, if they have ever even *seen me;* in other words, he thought, so long as I am not a ghost—they will immediately know that something is different, and that this difference is the backpack. I would never wear a backpack, Harold thought, or any other kind of strapped bag: it was unseemly, un*man*ly. A man should be able to subsist on nothing but his own will, he thought, with no need for a backpack, or anything of the sort. Backpacks are vulgar, he thought, staring at the black hole; they are frankly obscene. And even if his colleagues didn't notice the backpack specifically—because wearing strapped bags as a man had become, like all of the most detestable behaviors, "normalized"—they should still, Harold thought, at least, *sense* that something had changed.

Harold hadn't used a backpack since he was a child;

even in high school he had opted for a briefcase. It was a risk, Harold knew—the only other kid who carried a briefcase in school was frail and boogery, and had gas attacks in class—but Harold had played sports in middle school, which had been recent enough in his classmates' memories that he still retained some credibility. People still thought he was cool, even if a little strange. The briefcase, he'd calculated, would be forgiven by his would-be tormentors, due to his proximity to them in their memory. By slandering Harold with any number of epithets he'd rehearsed as possibilities—"briefcase boy," "office monkey"—they would implicate themselves, since Harold had so recently been one of them. Backpacks, those sticky pits of jumbled stuff, he thought, fondling his newfound acquisition, should be illegal. Backpacks made everyone look like turtles, or mules—like *peasants*, Harold thought—and there was no way that his colleagues wouldn't immediately notice his new peasantlike demeanor.

Harold bent his neck a bit to see the corner of the poster, peeking out from beneath the table.

Panicked, but at a distance, like he was worried on behalf of someone else, he wondered, in half sentences, what constituted a "marginalized identity," while also fearing, at any moment, Dolly's arrival.

Harold took his phone out of his pocket and looked down, alternating between the screen, the corner of the poster, and the backpack, then resolved to look straight down at the floor, in hopes that if Dolly entered and saw him staring straight down at the ground, she would leave.

Harold scratched his head. He swatted at his shirt and watched the dandruff swirl midair, some suspended there in fluorescent light, which, unlike natural light—the kind of light that caused his dandruff to appear snow-like, even beautiful—made it appear papery and gross. But even this reminded him of Dolly.

When Dolly first joined the department, she arrived during a snowstorm, and, in an attempt to make small talk, Harold had asked her whether or not, coming from her hometown, she'd seen much snow. Her face contorted into an appalled gasp, like he had accidentally confessed to something grave, then reconfigured itself into a rigid, forced composure. Her eyes scanned Harold's body slowly, then stopped at his face and held his eyes as he looked away. She laughed one short burst, like a cough.

"Not everywhere in the South is the same," she said, stonily. "It *snows* there too."

Her teeth showed when she talked, like she was chewing meat. She flipped her hair. Harold could tell that he had made a grievous mistake. He'd tried to find something pleasant, something broad to bring them together—her hometown and the weather—but he had accidentally stumbled upon an irreconcilable difference between them.

Harold tried to smile and attempted a joke about how he was surprised, because he had always thought "everywhere in the South was the same," but his voice betrayed him: he did not successfully convey that he was joking. Instead, as he frequently reflected in the subsequent years, he must have sounded like he was mocking her. He'd even fabricated a version of the memory in which he'd affected a Southern accent as he said it, convinced that this was the only thing that could possibly explain her instantaneous disdain toward him. Dolly did not laugh or return his smile. She cleared her throat and looked past him with far eyes.

There are moments in life when time touches eternity, when the significance of even the smallest detail is imbued with its true nature, and everything becomes vivid and torturously still. Harold was frozen in this single moment with Dolly forever. There was no possibility, no hope—only stabbing, awkward pain.

Eventually, another of their colleagues, Sarah, had walked by and introduced herself, and Dolly's demeanor had changed entirely; she dramatically turned her whole torso away from Harold. Harold said goodbye and skittered off.

After this miserable encounter things had only gotten worse. Harold could not find a way to connect. He mulled it over, tried different approaches, but nothing seemed to work: their initial encounter had infected the rest. Not knowing why things had gone so poorly, and knowing in more lucid moments that he had not, in fact, affected a mock-Southern accent, he attributed this disconnect to the fact that he had brought up the weather. Something about the weather where Dolly was from, he reasoned, must have caused his mentioning it to make her thoroughly dislike him right away.

Snowstorms were rare at Shepherd College, which is why in retrospect it seemed ominous that there had been one upon Dolly's arrival. However, despite the general lack of snow, the weather did get cold enough that one could not comfortably do anything outside; it became frigid and blustery, the grass and trees and buildings frozen, skies gray; but there was no beautiful snow to look at. Where Harold was from, the winters were severe, and cut through any pretense one might have had about oneself in warmer seasons. The bitter winds made everyone turn inward. But as people turned inward, they also turned out toward each other: there was nothing else to keep one's mind off the cold. Where Harold was from, the below-freezing temperatures and feet of snow destroyed any performance, and everyone bonded over this frigidity—from which they attempted to find relief in each other. When two bodies suffered cold, they came together to make heat, even if this just meant talking to take their minds off it.

So after Harold bungled this first encounter with Dolly, which had haunted all their consequent encounters, he'd begun to defensively consider "the weather," especially in moments when he felt bad for other reasons. People thought that mentioning the weather was thin and amateurish, he thought, shortly after a story he wrote that contained a line about the winters in his hometown got rejected by a major publication, when in reality it was actually one of the best subjects to talk about. In our disparate and degraded culture, Harold thought, staring at the rejection email, where we no longer have anything in common, making reference to the weather is a gesture toward something we share, something that transcends petty differences. Mentioning the weather provided a frame to commiserate, share gratitude, tell a story; on that fateful day, Harold considered, the snow had fallen on both Harold and Dolly the same.

However, mentioning the weather had proved fatal. Dolly, perhaps because of the lack of snow where she was from, Harold supposed, or something else, had decided to engage him in a perpetual, strategic conversation-dance to which he did not know the moves. Each of her phrases seemed carefully calculated based on some outside arithmetic: she said one thing but meant another, and the whole time Harold thought of snow.

Harold's awareness was brought back to the room as he realized he'd been absently pinching and pulling his shirt, watching dandruff fly and circle in the air, then land back on him. He put his hands at his side and stared blurrily now at the corner of the "marginalized identities" poster, feeling Dolly maliciously approaching from behind.

An individual can perform their group identity so thinly and obnoxiously, he thought, that it might make a more integrated individual wonder whether or not he actually hates that group of people as a whole.

Harold's mind became sharp, as it occasionally did when he "fasted," like a knife, and he imagined, with an enormous amount of enthusiasm, that he was getting interviewed about Dolly on a podcast he'd been listening to recently.

Dolly is an identity performer, Harold thought, envisioning himself talking into a mic. She is a performer of *Southernness*, Harold thought. Three months after

Dolly joined the faculty, Harold thought-talked, imagining the podcast host nodding along, I found myself wondering whether or not I harbored some secret animosity toward Southerners in general. Of course, he thought-talked, this was absurd: I do not hate Southerners; I don't even dislike Southerners; in fact, I like Southerners much more than most Northern people I know.

Harold generally liked the American South. But he had to be careful praising the South on a podcast. The American South could have been great, he thought, but now his mind went blank; his mind was like cheese that had become unpleasantly soft and, Harold imagined, smelly. Harold was hungry. If Dolly came in now, he thought, she'd smell his mind and interrupt his podcast rehearsal. He needed to focus while he still had the chance.

The American South could have been great, he continued, had it not immediately become a parody of itself after the Civil War. To non-Southerners, the American South became a caricature, he thought, and then continued caricaturing itself until all that was left was a complete and total satire, an *earnest satire*, he thought-talked, pausing to ponder the phrase "earnest satire," which had surprised him. The South became a caricatured version of *The South* that was in reality devoid of all things Southern, and which still existed as a kind of coping mechanism for having lost the war.

Harold imagined that the podcast host was losing interest. It was easy for an academic to lose a podcast host's interest, and it was even easier to be misunderstood if he was not sufficiently disapproving of something commonly understood to be evil. People wanted quips and stories and sound bites; they wanted clear-cut moral lines, like cocaine on a mirror.

For example, he thought-talked, I love new pop country music. Many people hate new pop country music, and they hate new pop country music because it sounds like a parody of old country music, but country music has always been a parody, he thought-talked, because the South, which produced country music, has always been a parody of itself, at least since after the war, when their identity became indelibly associated with slavery—and losing—and they could never recover, or separate themselves from the stain of not only evil but also losing.

It is one thing to be evil, Harold thought-talked, but it is another thing to be an evil *loser*, and this is what the South was to the North.

In America, Harold thought, the South wasn't haunted by an evil spirit but by a loser spirit, which is what had caused such disgust for its customs.

In the South, Harold thought-talked, you encounter that strange combination of guilt and pride that occurs when you end up on the wrong side of something, and this becomes synonymous with your identity to outsiders, such that you're always saying "I'm sorry" and "screw you" at the same time.

The natural landscape in the South is still beautiful, Harold thought-talked, even if the hills sloped too steeply in places, and the green seemed to run with rust and blood. Seen from a car, or otherwise secluded enough from its cretinous inhabitants to appreciate it, the South was magnificent. Although, of course, Harold thought-talked, imagining the podcast hosts in front of him and Dolly approaching from behind, *not everywhere in the South is the same.* The people can be wooden-headed and even slow, Harold thought-talked, but Southerners—who are no longer really Southerners but rather phantom Southerners, Harold thought-talked, or images of Southerners—are still steeped, however weakly, in some form of a tradition, even if it has survived only in a bloated and mangled and fundamentally symbolic form. The American South is, Harold thought, due to this remnant of tradition, entirely misunderstood by the North, who hates tradition, and so hates the South, and by extension hates Southerners.

Harold was now grateful for Dolly's imminent appearance—he felt productive. This was the most important work he'd done all week. He was "organizing his thoughts," so that, by the time he finally wrote another book or essay that required him to make podcast appearances, he'd be better prepared to speak extemporaneously.

In the past, Harold thought-talked, Americans could work a normal job and feed their families; but now, Harold thought, the jobs were gone, and the American economy was changing. America no longer produced material goods. The American Dream was to get a fake computer job; to become a "knowledge worker"; to become a part of the new aristocracy of brains; to sit in front of a laptop, sending emails.

But the South, with few exceptions, was stuck in this in-between time, a kind of non-time, in which people still yearned for the real—but could not find it. The agriculture has been destroyed, and the manufacturing, what little of it there was, had been exported; and all that was left, in the end, was television and fast food, in addition to remnants of Christianity, which had stuck around in such a zombified form that Flannery O'Connor had once quipped that the South was, Harold thought-talked while looking at the backpack's zippers, not "Christ-centered" so much as "Christ-haunted."

In spite of itself, however, and despite the Northern scorn, Harold thought, the South had still managed to produce a fair amount of good.

Harold tried to block out the thought of Dolly coming down the hall. What was taking her so long? He imagined kneeling before her and slowly slipping her shoes off when she sat down—then hitting her with them.

Harold stared at the corner of the "marginalized identities" poster with unfocused eyes. Often, what people call their identity is not their identity at all, Harold thought-talked, but rather a costume for what is ultimately their performance; they become possessed by this performance until they can't tell the difference between their performance and themselves. They construct glistening, labyrinthian ideologies that claim, always convolutedly, that every identity is a performance, and this is only to justify their weasely falseness; there is no longer any distinction between one's performance and one's personhood.

A life lived honestly, Harold thought, was not concerned with eliciting particular responses from an audience. One should not always be trying to manipulate others into perceiving them a certain way, Harold thought-talked, feeling Dolly behind him, and yet Dolly is aggressively trying to manipulate me, Harold thought, trying to get me to think Southerner, instead of Dolly, even now.

Dolly is from a small town in the South, and everything about her, everything she says and does, Harold thought-talked, is a small-town-in-the-South performance. (On the podcast, would Harold call Dolly "Dolly" or "my colleague"? Or would he call her "Vance" or "Sarah" or some other name?)

When Dolly first joined the Shepherd faculty, he continued, she talked often about the differences between our school and the school she had come from—the differences between Shepherd College and Bardley Community College—and, ultimately, about the differences between the North and the South. In reality, Shepherd was in the South, Harold corrected himself—Shepherd College was technically the northernmost part of the South—but it was not *Dolly's South* and so was, to her, the North.

But, Harold thought, feeling energized, even if Shepherd was in the North, and not the northernmost part of the South, it wouldn't matter: there was no authentic difference between the North and the South, just as there was no authentic difference between small towns and cities, because everything had become homogenized due to the internet and the market.

Yes, Harold thought, he would invoke "the market" . . .

Dolly lives forty minutes away from Shepherd, Harold thought-talked, whereas I live thirty-five minutes away. Harold paused, considering that he would never actually say this on a podcast, and would very likely never mention Dolly on a podcast at all, except to maybe say that they were colleagues, or to nod and agree when someone else was praising her. Dolly lives in what is considered a *real city*, he thought-talked, whereas I live in the land of politicians and journalists, which is to say the land of fakers and schemers. It is absolutely Dolly's style, Harold thought-talked, to drive forty minutes—fifty-five minutes in traffic—each day, so that she can say she lives in a *real city*; to drive fifty-five minutes to and from work each day in traffic in order to say she *likes her neighborhood* and *likes her apartment.*

I hate my neighborhood and I hate my apartment, Harold thought. He touched the poster peeking out from the roping wood with the rubber sole of his shoe. He lightly flicked it with his foot.

Whenever Dolly mentioned her neighborhood or her apartment, Harold thought, she always very quickly mentioned the cheap rent. *It's so much more affordable here*, she'd say. *My funky hip-oh*—she liked to put "oh" at the end of words, which one of their colleagues, to Harold's dismay, had begun to call a "Dollyism"—*apartment in my funky hip-oh neighborhood is so much cheaper than the lame-oh neighborhoods thirty-five minutes in the other direction from Shep-herd, but it's still not as cheap-oh as back home.*

Dolly's lips were always flapping with an anecdote about *back home* and her *kin*. She drawled on about how she felt like a *fish on a plate of baked beans* and how *Jesus was a socialist* and how *not everywhere in the South is the same.*

Dolly pretends to love the South, Harold thought-talked, but in reality she hates the South. He thought he heard the door behind him. He flinched.

Dolly grew up in the South, Harold thought-talked frantically, and she presents herself as being from a small Southern town, but in reality she is a middling urban elite disguised as a Southerner. Dolly presents herself as having been from a small Southern town, he thought-talked, when in reality she grew up in the large coastal city of her heart and her brain. She has none of the same beliefs as the people she grew up with, none of the same ideas or respect for tradition; she has no understanding of the customs or values of her people; she did not vote for their president and she does not worship their god. In short, Harold thought-talked, convinced now that she was behind him, Dolly grew up hating her environment and the people around her; she grew up hating everything they loved, and she set out in life—made it her mission in life—to destroy them.

Dolly wanted nothing but to destroy the South while saying "I love the South" and "I grew up in the South" with a smile.

Harold closed his eyes and tried not to move.

Dolly moved to a Northern city, got a degree in

gender studies with a minor in creative writing, moved back home, and got a job at a community college with the intention of enlightening the people—*her people*—but then, discovering that they did not want to be enlightened, she left and got a job at Shepherd College; she moved to a farther-north-but-still-technically-Southern city, and has since made it her mission to destroy our departmental meetings with her pseudo-South performance, and to eventually destroy the entire American South with her Northern progressivism, Harold thought. All her life, Dolly envied the North. She resented the South and wanted to turn the South into the North; Dolly wanted to turn everything into a city. And now that she lives in a city, Harold thought-talked, where she really belongs and where she really is from, she pretends to be from the South and to love the South, all as a part of her ultimate plan to destroy the South, and not only to destroy the South but to destroy the North too. Dolly is only Southern insofar as she is a parody. She is, in short, Harold thought, a South-obliterator, and her whole life is a small-South-town charade. Her Southernness was a gaudy garment, disguising everything that might have been real and true and good about her. Dolly's South was not the South but a waffle maker, mushing all the disparate parts of Dolly into a South-waffle—flat and predictably ridged.

Harold curled his neck around his chair, expecting to find Dolly standing there with murderous rage in her eyes.

He was alone.

VI

SOUTH-OBLITERATOR, SOUTH-MURDERER, HAR-
old wrote in the Notes app on his phone, feeling
clammy, even sticky, thinking of the closing image
from Dolly's most recent novel: a trail of dead bodies leading to a heap of piled corpses steaming in the
Southern heat. Her novel, which featured countless
unsolved murders, was received by the media as a great
step forward for literature written by women: men
had always written books about murder and death, violence and war; now, women could write about them
too. Before, only men could end their novels with a
twenty-page description of the smell and sight of siz-
zling piled corpses in the sun; now women could also
succeed in meticulously depicting charred and blister-
ing remains. "Women have been waiting for this opportunity," one reviewer wrote, "for centuries."

Despite Dolly's continued absence, Harold still felt an acute sense of being pursued. He wanted to flee. He looked down at the backpack. Then he got up.

Harold pushed the heavy doors and walked out into the hall, now mostly empty; his feet took him directly toward a corkboard, where he paused: flyers, blurry images, a piece of paper that said MENTAL HEALTH, MENTAL WEALTH with clip-art dollar signs and brains around it, and paper slips at the bottom with a phone number one could tear off and take. Most of them were gone. Next to it was a line drawing of the lower half of a woman's naked body, and a poem beneath that read:

> *Your silence will not save you*
> *and neither will your denial*
> *Lesbians have always been*
> *everywhere. GAY REALITY.*

Harold flinched as he felt a bug fly past his ear, but when he turned he saw that it was just a student walking quickly. The student nearly tripped over himself, carrying an armful of papers.

"Watch where you're going," Harold growled, but the student was long past Harold now, and he spoke too quietly for anyone to hear.

Harold glanced at the lesbian art exhibit flyer again. Harold's hunger set his teeth on edge. His temples pulsed, like a heartbeat; he unhinged his jaw, flashing his cavernous mouth quickly before it set back to its normal, clenched position. A student passed, eating a donut, and he remembered that there was a little stand somewhere in Lawes that sold granola bars and cold, plastic-wrapped sandwiches. Harold had passed it a few times when it was closed, so he'd only ever passively registered its existence as vague shapes. He was terribly hungry, and unsure how to get there, but he went where his feet took him, discerning the directions intuitively, taking a left, then a right, then going straight, then right again.

Harold's head seemed to leak out of itself; it seeped into the corridors, such that his experience of walking through Lawes was like moving through his own mind; he came back into awareness of his surroundings when he accidentally bumped into Vance. Startled, Harold looked up, then immediately cast his eyes downward, past Vance's short torso and long legs, and apologized. "How . . . God I'm . . . I'm trying to get to the snack stand, and . . ." Harold said. But, just as Harold expected, Vance gawked at him, albeit with penetrating eyes, as if Harold were a text and Vance were trying to read him.

"Snack stand," Harold said, growing impatient. "The stand . . ." Would he be forced to repeat "snack stand" to Vance? Would he be forced to suffer the indignity of explaining "snack stand" to someone so self-evidently lesser than him?

Vance looked into Harold's face. "Hm, mm," Vance said. "Which one?"

This was too much for Harold. Of course Vance would ask "which one," when it was perfectly clear what Harold was referring to. Were there multiple snack stands in Lawes? Vance is trying to make me pay, Harold thought, for bumping into him . . . *Which one?* Harold was filled with a contemptuous glee. He kept his eyes on the floor, apologized again, and reached out to clasp Vance's hand, shaking it and patting it gingerly with his free hand, like a beggar.

As they departed, Harold was suddenly in a fine mood. Harold concocted a plan—he would lock eyes with Vance during the meeting and hold his gaze. There was no question about it now. Harold had Vance right where he wanted him. Harold took another couple of turns, finding himself lost now in the Lawes halls, moving passively, as if possessed. He hadn't exacted his revenge—not yet. He hadn't held Vance's eyes, but he would hold them in the meeting, and it would be all the more effective because everyone would see him dominating Vance, and Vance wouldn't see it coming. Vance would be worn out by this Pyrrhic victory, having assumed that he had conquered Harold simply by asking *which one* in such a numbskulled tone. The meeting would be the final round, and, until then, Harold would conserve his energy. He just needed to eat, then everything would come together and work to Harold's advantage.

Harold's legs carried him confidently, but he did not know where he was going.

After more dizzying turns, Harold entered an unfamiliar hall: if he had been there before, it was unrecognizable now; there were caution tape X's on all the wooden doors. Harold took a deep breath; the hall looked exactly like the hall where his classroom was located, with only a few minor differences. Harold touched the crown of his head with his fingertips. The hall looked like a giant, artificial womb; Harold dragged his fingers against the wall as he walked.

There was a piece of paper taped to one of the doors in the distance. Harold looked around. Was he alone? Where was everyone? The paper displayed a written statement; Harold scanned it and discerned that there had been a "leak" that had left the "northwest hall un-inhabitable." Harold squinted intently at the letter. He couldn't tell if it was handwritten or typed. The penmanship was too consistent to be written by hand, but still somehow not perfect enough to be made by a machine. Harold heard a loud creak, like a groan—and he jumped. Smiling and quivering, he reapproached the piece of paper and touched it with his right hand. At the end of the unsigned letter, the anonymous author thanked everyone for their patience while the school "swiftly dealt with this unfortunate matter."

The paper was stuck to the doorframe with blue masking tape at the top, but the bottom fluttered, as if blown by gentle wind. The deep-brown door was lightly scratched, as if an animal had clawed it, revealing lighter wood beneath. The air in the hall was still—Harold imagined licking his pointer finger and lifting it up in the air to confirm, something he vaguely recalled seeing in a film adaptation of *Sherlock Holmes*—yet the paper still moved. Was the wind coming from inside the room? Perhaps someone had left a window open inside, and there was a hole in the wood beneath the paper, making it move?

Harold lifted the bottom of the paper—solid wood.

What did I expect? Harold thought, relieved, nearly laughing. Some portal, or . . . He wanted there to be some tiny hole that he could peer into. He wanted to encounter something revelatory and unspeakable. How ridiculous! Harold stepped back, glancing at the word "uninhabitable," which lapped against the doorframe like a wave. Suddenly, the paper stilled. What was going on? Had Harold touched the paper unknowingly, making it move? All at once, Harold felt cold, and the caution-taped doors seemed to multiply. He was alone in the endlessly X'd hall. He skittered around the corner, back the way he came, and sank down against the wall.

He checked his phone. Eleven minutes left until the meeting. How was this even possible? Harold clicked his teeth.

At Shepherd College, time moved differently than in the outside world. It was a cliché that life in the academy was somehow separate from "real life," and, as with most clichés, it was true: at Shepherd, the walls and floors and ceilings absorbed time and postponed "life"—a kind of purgatory—but instead of offering in return education, erudition, refinement, vitality, or even a career, as those vultures with vested interests promised, the floors and walls and ceilings sucked up time and spit out death. If the academy was purgatory, everyone eventually ended up in the same place.

Whatever leak there was had hopefully already been dealt with, Harold thought. If it was so severe, why wasn't there caution tape preventing him from entering the area altogether? Why hadn't Harold received an "alert to inspire" email, or even just a regular alert about the leak? What kind of leak could it even have been? Gas? *Me?* Harold thought. He grinned.

I have always been curious, Harold thought. I am an academic. I am a snoop. I am an academic—and a snoop; but I repeat myself! I really should have packed a lunch.

Harold left the dark hall and stumbled back the way he'd come. He couldn't remember the path he had taken, but he walked with purpose, hoping to encounter something that might direct him. Harold thought again of his first campus visit, when, as he stumbled incoherently around the basement, he felt as if he'd already experienced everything that would happen to him there, like a premonition. It was as if Harold were dead, and looking back on his life from the future. Time was collapsing. The past existed in the present; the future felt like a hazy memory.

Harold smelled flowers decomposing, fleshy mass, oppressive heat—fear and revulsion, disorienting slabs of concrete, brick. Despite everything he'd learned and taught at Shepherd, there was nothing powerful enough to drown this other kind of knowing in him. It was as if his brain had access to all of life already, and when he was at Shepherd, he knew, like déjà vu, that this was what would destroy him. As Harold meandered back to where he came from, wondering whether or not he'd been exposed to some poisonous gas, he had a sneaking sense that his life was predetermined, that there was nothing in his litany of days that could have happened any differently, both inside and outside of him—an inevitability that crushed even his strongest sense of self-determination. No matter how hard he fought against his crippled fate, he would always be in the clutches of some malevolent, tentacled beast; professors and students; the sinewy halls.

At Shepherd, the professors destroyed one another, as well as the students, and the bureaucrats were there to make sure it all got done. In addition to the "alert to inspire" emails, Harold had gotten a series of distressingly vague messages about some "reports" in the English Department, and was informed that he would be called in to "chat" at some later date, but he didn't know when, or with whom, or about what. In classic Shepherd fashion, he did not merely receive one email containing necessary information but many emails leading up to what would be the necessary email, such that he never knew which email would contain something actionable, and he'd have to parse multiple many-paragraphed emails in order to get any concrete details.

Harold arrived at the meeting room as if he'd been teleported there, shuffling unconsciously back to the same seat as before and dropping the backpack at his feet. Time converged upon him from all sides. In academia, death, as opposed to education, was the end. Academia was "separate from life," and what could be separate from life besides death?

A small group of students swung open the heavy door with ease and ambled in.

"Fu—" one said.

"Tttttt," said another. "Ohf."

When they saw Harold, they stopped.

"Is this . . ." one of the students said, looking at his friends. Had they been following him?

"Yes," said Harold. "Or—" He tried to think quickly. He reached down and awkwardly fondled the backpack.

"We're just a room," one of the students said. "Or"—he laughed—"we're looking for a room." His voice creaked. His head was shaved and his eyebrows were blond, nearly invisible.

"You can study here if you want," Harold said, then winced. Why did he say that? It had just fallen out of him. The students would have to leave when the meeting started, which was now fast approaching. Harold looked down at his phone. Nine minutes. He could pretend he'd forgotten about the meeting, he considered, and when his colleagues trickled in, the students would just naturally leave. Or, he thought, he could tell them right now that, actually, there was a meeting soon. They wouldn't care either way. He imagined standing up and barking at them: *Get out!*

He twisted up his face to try to repel them. "I won't bother you," he snarled.

"We don't need to study," the bald student said, eyeing the backpack. Harold was unthinkingly massaging it now, drawing attention to it. The other students caught the bald student's eyes and followed them down to the black mass on the floor.

Harold fingered a zipper, then placed his hands in his lap. "Is there anything I can help you with?" he asked.

"We're looking for something," said the bald student. The others fidgeted giddily.

Harold flexed his calves. He scooted the backpack even closer in toward himself with his right foot. "Actually," Harold said. "Wait, I just remembered." He flinched. "There's a meeting here soon."

The bald student was practically licking his lips at the backpack. His lips were still, but Harold could see that they were wet, and he guessed that the student had been licking them when Harold wasn't looking at him. Then another of the students, in a black T-shirt with a ponytail, spoke.

"Professor Harold?" he asked.

Harold's upper body became stiff.

"I took your Dostoevsky class. I used to be an English major." He paused, and reached behind his head to tighten his hair tie. "I'm studying business now, but with a minor in creative writing."

Harold didn't recognize the student. And he had never taught a Dostoevsky class. The student must have been thinking of David, who had taught a Dostoevsky class, and who, by all accounts, had butchered Dostoevsky like a cow. Rather, Harold had heard from one student that the class was "amazing," but, from the way the student spoke about it, Harold could tell that it had been a complete and total butchering. This ponytailed student had called him Professor Harold, though, so he did in fact know who he was ... Why had he said "Harold," when he so obviously meant "David"?

"Business and creative writing," Harold said dumbly. He wanted the students to leave. He wanted all of the students to leave. He wanted every single student at Shepherd College to disappear, and to never set foot on any college campus ever again. The students' eyes kept drifting toward the backpack. Did it belong to one of them? Or one of their friends? What were they looking for?

He should have paid closer attention to the people who were standing around the backpack before he took it. Harold tried to picture faces and bodies, but all he could remember were wide pants. One had seemed tall, he recalled, and one had been missing an arm. No. Harold was remembering a movie he'd seen recently, with the arm. Was one wearing a suit? No— Harold could not remember anything about the students who had stood around the backpack. Did they even have faces?

"Business and creative writing," the student repeated. "I love writing, or, *creative* writing," he chuckled, "but it's important to know how to market yourself. Especially now. I took that class with Professor Dawkle about how to market yourself as a writer online. It was mostly about being a writer, but it's really a transferable skill to any discipline. Even beyond creative disciplines. I mean, I learned that I really love marketing. Everything is marketing. It was eye-opening. How it's important to b-b-" He paused. "Brand—"

"It's mine," Harold said softly, tapping his right foot on the backpack.

The ponytailed student, confused, now wore a sympathetic expression. Another of the students approached, looking down.

"Stop," Harold said. "Or, ahhh—" He coughed.

The student stared at Harold quizzically. He smelled like cigarettes and weed.

"Well, anyway, it was good to see you," the ponytailed student continued, somewhat hesitantly. "We'll get out of your way."

The student who approached Harold handed him a flyer for his art show. "One of the paintings is based on *The Idiot*," he said. "I thought, since you're a Dostoevsky scholar." He backed away.

Harold detected a subtle smirk on the student's face. Did he know that Harold was not a Dostoevsky scholar? Was this student calling him an idiot?

"We can go back to my place," one of the students said. "I don't have class for the next five days. And I'm pretty sure . . ."

The students became a distant murmur as they exited the heavy doors.

Harold heard a laugh. It echoed.

When they were gone, Harold shot up and pressed his ear against the door, trying to listen for their footsteps, but he couldn't hear any one thing, only a humming mass. They were sure to return, Harold thought, perhaps with a security guard, or the dean—or even a real police officer, since Harold had committed a real—no, he wouldn't let himself think it. If they returned, so be it. But still, it would be best for him not to have his head pressed up against the door, in case they did swing it open, especially with the force of a cop or an angry administrator, knowing he was in there, cracking into his head and toppling him over like a Greek or Roman statue. These weasels were always waiting for their day of glory, when they could finally have an excuse to topple someone like him . . .

Harold reached down and gripped the backpack. He needed to get rid of it. He didn't want it anymore. *If you want it, you can have it!* Harold started shivering. The administration had installed many new cameras on campus due to the recent uptick in theft, but, based on his memory, there wasn't a camera in the hall where he had taken the backpack; if he got rid of it now, there'd be no proof. It would be his word against the students', and who would they believe: Harold, a veritable *professor of English*, or a gangly group of mentally defective students—one with a bald head and barely visible eyebrows? Harold closed his eyes and tried to imagine a camera in the area he'd taken the backpack from. He imagined corners where the ceiling met the wall, and tried to picture little machine arms with tiny boxlike camera hands. There was an app, which a student organization, Equity for All, had created, where one could see the locations of all the new cameras, but Harold didn't know if he'd have time to download it before they all returned to confront him.

Equity for All, he thought with disgust. The group, predicting that the new security measures would disproportionately affect people of color, opposed the cameras, filming themselves confronting the workers who were installing them, shouting "Murderer! Murderer!" and "White supremacist spies have no place at Shepherd College!" In one lengthier video, a white woman with a greasy mullet shoved a camera in a Mexican technician's face, asking, in a menacing tone, if he were to "peel his skin off," would she "find white underneath?"

MANY OF THE professors and administrators attributed the thefts to the students' needs not being met. "How can anyone learn anything," one had said, "when they're not sure where their next meal is coming from?" No one with a full belly and a roof over their head and healthcare has ever committed a crime, Harold thought.

Shepherd cost $60,000 per year. It was the banks, Harold thought, who gave huge loans to people like the freaks who'd just come in, and the college—which had increased tuition fourfold in four decades—who were the real thieves. As for the relatively minor thefts on campus, people didn't need a reason to hurt each other, Harold thought—they needed a reason not to.

But then again, Harold was hungry when he'd taken the backpack. Maybe there was something to the theory after all.

Harold pictured the bald student. In recent years, it was not uncommon for half the class or more to drop out of his Gothic novel seminar once they learned about the workload: they read one novel every other week and had to write two four-page papers. This was not even a fourth of the work he'd had to do when he was in school, but it was significantly more than what many of his colleagues assigned.

The same group that protested the camera installations had, with the support of the new administrators, revised school codes to be more amenable to students who struggled financially, or mentally, or in any other way, such that the students, and not the professors—and not even the students, but the worst students—were in charge. College is for the students' benefit, they reasoned, and so the college should take the students' needs into account. College wasn't only for the best—or rather, *most privileged*—students; college was for all students, all people, and it needed to create more equitable outcomes, always.

People are equal, Harold thought, parroting Dolly in a departmental meeting months prior, and so any disparate outcome must necessarily be rooted in some form of injustice.

Are people not equal? he thought, imagining himself as Dolly. Are people not equal, Harold?

Although the noise outside the door was lawlessly indeterminate, Harold heard beneath it marching boots, even an engine. It was only a matter of time before they stormed into the room and took him away.

Harold inched away from the door, dragging his legs behind him on the ground.

If they took him, he would not go easily. He would have his say. If they made a big enough scene, a student, likely multiple students, would film it. He could use it as an opportunity to give an impassioned speech, to state his case.

"Why are you here?" he'd shriek at all those holding phones. "We all know you're *supposed* to be here," he'd shout. "But why?" He'd rub his pointer finger up and down on his thumb with the rest of his fingers clamped down on his palm. "Is it an investment? An investment? Well . . . it's a terrible investment. Or how about a vacation?" Depending on which way they took him, it was possible they'd pass the giant sign that advertised the new dining hall, as well as some other sparkling flourishes Shepherd had added to the campus recently, to enhance "student life": large pictures of groups of students laughing and smiling; an image of a swimmer, with the text "Discover Yourself" beneath it.

"An investment vacation," Harold would yell at the students holding phones, "who ever heard of that? You think college will get you a job; it won't get you a job. You invest in your future by going into debt to learn nothing from people who hate themselves. So you invest in your future by going on vacation—but it's the worst vacation of all time, for what it costs . . ."

Harold imagined fighting off security and his colleagues. "Unless this is all just insurance? Shepherd: could save you fifteen years of living destitute on the streets of a major city in exchange for $240,000 and four years of your life? The cracks in society are growing larger," Harold would yell, "and I am your insurance agent!"

Harold pulled his feet around his side and sat up straight now, pretzel-legged.

"You think Shepherd really *cares*?" he would yell. "Look what they're doing to me!" He'd bare his teeth. "I vant to suck!"

Harold checked his phone. Six and a half minutes left. Investment . . . Vacation . . . Insurance . . . The gym . . . He tapped his foot and checked his email. Nothing. He got up off the floor and went back to the table. Surely they would take him now, before the meeting? It was likely beyond even their capacity for evil to confront him about the backpack in front of everyone at the meeting. Shepherd liked to do these things behind the scenes.

Ah. This last thought stilled his head. Of course they wouldn't just bust into the room and drag him kicking and screaming through the halls! That would reflect just as poorly on Shepherd as it would on Harold. After the stabbing, Shepherd couldn't afford another controversy.

The floor beneath Harold's feet began to pulse, causing his right leg to shake. His mind was scattered and sharp, like broken glass. Throngs of students in halls; brain fog. The shifting, swelling floor beneath Harold gripped him, and he was overtaken by the sense that soon the students would burst up from below, resurrected, so to speak, to punish him for what the college—and Harold as one of its appendages—had done.

Harold kicked the backpack. You can handle this, he thought. You got this.

Okay. Okay. Harold took a breath. He nestled into his stiff chair, but the floor sent shooting pains up through his legs; he lifted them, and started to stomp rhythmically, lifting his right then left leg, stomping each foot on the floor, alternating, though sometimes stomping both together, all while humming to get the voices from the hall out of his head—all he wanted, *needed*, was a moment of peace before his meeting.

Harold executed these movements imperceptibly, and hummed, he thought, so quietly that no one who entered the room would be able to hear. The door opened and closed. Harold turned around. Nothing. Harold tried to breathe into his feet.

Harold pressed his tongue against the backs of his teeth. He clenched his fists and flexed his forearms, trying to gauge his relative strength compared with other days. He felt weak. His stomach gurgled. He glanced at his forearm veins.

Strength, Harold thought, was the king of all virtues. His forearm veins were not as pronounced as they had been when he was leaner, but he could still see them, rising in his skin the harder and longer he flexed. His arm itched. He decided not to scratch it. Let it itch, he thought. Let it itch.

He scratched it.

He looked down and saw that he had smeared a mosquito on his arm. Blood and little bits of bug were squished into his arm hair. He rubbed the mosquito pieces until they fell onto the floor. Harold hated these meetings; he hated these ostensible "discussions" and "updates"; he hated being crammed into a room and forced to talk, or listen, about this or that update, this or that change, when in reality there was never a change, or an update, but a variation of the same things said in every meeting prior. When people come together, Harold thought, inspecting his arm hairs for bloody bits of bug, there is always the possibility that something truly beautiful might occur, but, at Shepherd . . .

Harold lifted his phone off the table, then checked his email, again. He clicked a new email, which had been sent to all the faculty, informing them that the meeting would now take place in room 1010, instead of the room Harold was in, so that they could use one of the new projectors.

Ffff . . . Gfhfff . . . 1010, 1010, Harold thought.

Harold got up and stumbled through Lawes. The walls appeared fleshlike and the doors like vacant, wooden eyes.

VII

THE ROOM WAS ALIVE.

Almost everything was identical to the other room: the white walls, the white ceiling . . .

"Fff—" Harold clutched at his ribs. There was Vance, and John, and Sarah; there was Robin, and Brandon, and Ken.

Harold scanned the many faces that had tortured him intermittently for years, faces like feet, kicking him, for nearly a decade now. Harold was surrounded by feet-heads, nostrils flared like spread-out toes, gaping mouths sucking up what was meant for all of them to share, breathing out little kicks. The chairs, table, walls, and floor became a pulsing purple-red, like a suffocating face. The room and those in it merged into one giant organism. Harold made his way toward a chair.

Maybe this will help me build more endurance for

workouts, Harold considered, choking as he inhaled. He thought of a guy at his gym who exercised with a gas-mask-like contraption on his face: black straps wrapped around the back of his head; black plastic oval with slats, like bars, and a logo of a mountain, over his mouth. It's not every day that you find yourself surrounded by oxygen hogs, Harold thought, and in a situation where you can't breathe because of a severe lack of oxygen due to oxygen hogs with feet for heads. No. This will not help my muscles. Harold grimaced. Muscles needed oxygen to grow, and Harold could already feel his atrophying, withering into flat, limp sacks.

At least, Harold thought, he had L-citrulline and beetroot powder in the car, which would help oxygenate his blood before the workout.

Harold bent his neck toward each of his colleagues as their eyes met. Bend neck, eye contact, bend neck, take out phone, put phone back into pocket, try not to look pained, try not to throw up, try not to throw anything, don't shriek. He closed his eyes and tried to pray, *God*, but then he heard a voice—undoubtedly his—which started as a vague feeling of resistance, then burst forth with a forceful *No*.

Harold's eyes swiveled in their sockets toward Dolly's and David's pale faces as they staggered into the room. David's thin limbs flopped and wiggled. Dolly's voice rang out, bouncing back and forth between Harold's ears. He twisted his lips into a smile.

David—whose presence Harold felt behind him, like the past—was an associate professor whom the college had hired shortly after him. When David had come into Harold's office on his first day, he had immediately commented on a book, which lay open on Harold's desk: one of a three-volume anthology exploring René Girard's theory of "underground psychology," containing essays on everything from Nietzsche's relationship with Wagner to neuroscientific studies about addiction, occult studies, and poetry. The anthology was appropriately titled *Underground Psychology*. David hadn't read the book, but he'd heard of it, he assured Harold, in a bumbling, feverish manner, like he was confessing something that had been pent up. David said that the anthology seemed "interesting," but he could not understand why the editor hadn't included Harold's own work.

Harold couldn't tell whether this was meant to be a compliment or a slight. His body of work had been broadly misunderstood by many to be about this "underground"—a psychological state best illustrated in Dostoevsky's *Notes from Underground*, from which the condition got its name—but Harold didn't conceive of it this way. Harold disagreed with the characterization of himself, as one scholar put it, as "the most lucid underground scholar"; he disagreed with it so much that it consumed him for months after the phrase had first been published (despite the fact that only ten or so people had likely read the piece, which had been published in an academic journal and cost $35.95 to read)—yet, he too had wondered why his work was not included in the anthology that lay on his desk when David had first come to see him.

Harold's dissertation, which turned into his first academic book, began as an analysis of novels about exceptional men in societies that punished them. Society, particularly in the West, existed solely to keep exceptional men from living out their destiny; society had enacted its revenge upon the strong and vital, those individuals who, dreaming of something greater than daily toil, dared to envision new possibilities, to go out and take what was theirs, to create something new. The explosion of resentment among the masses—which reached its peak with Christianity but was already present in Judaism—became so hegemonic that these exceptional men, already few and far between, were like magnificent, rare seeds planted in bad soil: they could not flourish; they grew, and became deformed. The novels Harold was interested in showed what became of these men in a world where they could not *act*—they became absurd. But it was really the world that was absurd, Harold thought, and not these men.

Of course, Harold did not write his own thoughts directly into the work: he instead explored "A Nietzschean Reading of Dostoevsky," and "The Talented Mr. Schopenhauer," and so on. He even, at times, framed his own writing as a critique of what he intended to promote. He was an esotericist, he consoled himself, and so, despite his attempt to conceal his true views in his work, those in the know, he hoped, would understand. It was prudent for an academic to conceal themselves in their work, and to hide behind the words of someone long dead, to twist their words to fit their own purposes. Dead philosophers and authors were not philosophers and authors but rather wet rags wrung dry and placed over the mouths of academics, such that everything they said was filtered through them. If anyone misunderstood, the academic could simply point to the damp rag.

Harold's work was little-cited, and didn't sell. People had talked and written about it initially, but always with qualifications, and then they seemed to lose interest. Through cryptically valorizing these *exceptional men against society*, he felt like he was taking part in their struggle: through reading and writing about them, he had begun to view himself as one of them, and so it was only natural that his work would be met with a silent disdain. The only thing mediocrities hated more than bad people was exceptional people. This unsatisfying reaction from academia had been somewhat expected, but Harold couldn't help but wish his work had at least garnered more *negative* attention. This would have proven his thesis undeniably, and would have been endlessly gratifying—but it didn't happen.

It wasn't until his novel was published—about an artist who goes on a residency in rural Italy and kills another resident—that some reviewers in popular magazines engaged with his work. Finally, Harold thought, when it began generating some buzz, my blackened flowers. But the flowers he received were bright and normal. Reviewers called him a "master satirist"; the novel was a "comic portrayal of the reactionary right"; it was even a "novel about the myth of the exceptional man against society." In short, Harold had been totally misunderstood. He'd begun to wonder if he'd subconsciously *meant* for the novel to come across this way—if, despite his convictions, he still wanted the approval of the ants he told himself he wanted to squish beneath his boot.

This was also when Harold began seeing the word "underground" associated with his work. It was ridiculous, Harold knew, but it still nagged him, so he spent the better part of two years studying the subject. He read every book that mentioned the word "ressentiment"; he studied myth and ancient religion; he even spent eight months reading psychology textbooks, only to become convinced that psychology had next to nothing to offer anyone who wanted to understand the human mind. Harold felt increasingly disturbed. Despite all these warnings, if one could call them warnings, he continued on in his pursuit.

David understood, he'd said, on the day he came into Harold's office, why the editor of *Underground Psychology* might have wanted to include this or that author *other than Harold*, but he could not, "unless I'm missing something," he'd said, "which I'm sure I am," he assured Harold, see why Harold's novel about the steppe warrior, "which is quite literally the typification of the underground itself," was not excerpted in the book, or why none of his academic work had been included.

This was the exact phrase he'd used, "the typification of the underground itself," and, in that moment, Harold knew that there would forever exist an impassable gulf between David and him.

Over the ensuing weeks, Harold had tried to

extend grace and generosity to David, whose every word and gesture was unbearably obtuse, and whose "typification of the underground itself" rang in his ears like tinnitus—but it was all in vain. Whereas Dolly had intentionally crafted her performance and was therefore totally predictable, David was controlled by his performance, because he didn't believe he was performing—thus, he was totally insane.

David had a long scar on his face that cut down from the top of his right cheek, over his lips, and onto his chin. In certain light, such as in a dimly lit restaurant, the scar seemed mysterious, but in the fluorescent light of Lawes it looked crusty. He had gotten it as a child, he said, when he tripped and fell down a hill into a creek, slashing his face on a large rock, then lying blacked out in the grass until his mother found him.

This was another problem with David, Harold thought: he was clumsy.

David's gangly, uncontrolled limbs gave the impression of a doll in the grip of a malicious child, flopping and twisting him aggressively. He had long arms and long legs, as well as long fingernails, in addition to a long neck, and long teeth, and so one never felt quite out of harm's way when one had the unfortunate curse of being in his company: the possibility of a scratch or an accidental touch was always at the forefront of one's mind.

David wanted to dominate his colleagues but had only ever succeeded in being dominated by them, and therefore paradoxically could rise among them. This was why, Harold suspected, David would get tenure, and he would not. For Harold, tenure was not tenure but a weasel certificate. David did not understand why Harold's work was not mentioned in the underground tome, and this lack of understanding caused Harold to understand everything about David, including why David would get tenure . . .

In literature, as in life, we often think that we are looking for someone to identify with, but when we encounter that with which we should most identify, we recoil.

People often said David and Harold looked alike, but Harold did not see the resemblance.

David, for one, Harold thought, had a head that smelled persistently of cheese—which Harold attributed to his scar—and his skin flaked so abundantly that he always looked as if he'd come in from the snow. Sometimes, the skin flakes would land on his scar, which was darker than the rest of his pasty white skin, so the gleaming flakes appeared like inverse freckles.

Once, after Casey won an award that both David and Casey had both been nominated for, David had found Casey reading on a bench in the courtyard outside Lawes, where Harold was also reading, tucked away in a corner, out of view, and Harold watched as David proceeded to compliment Casey profusely. However, when Casey responded in a befuddled, somewhat flustered manner, not meeting David's excitement—the result, Harold imagined, of being interrupted while reading—David turned red, and muttered, "These awards, you know, they're basically meaningless anyway," then laughed.

As he laughed, Harold had noticed that David's

face was stiff; it was only after the laugh that his face moved—his smile had been delayed, like in bad ventriloquism. Harold had discerned a flash of spite beneath David's eyes, as he backed away from Casey, tripping over himself, and falling flat onto his back, wriggling before getting up and, without looking at either Casey or Harold, who was still hidden in the bushes, skittering away.

Later that day, David found Harold in his office, and told him he thought that Casey's award-winning essay was an "absolute abomination." Harold nodded, although he hadn't read the article, while feeling repulsed, and his hatred for David increased each time he nodded against his will.

If you took David and put him in a vat of hot liquid and boiled him down, Harold thought, this anecdote would be all that remained.

In the meeting room now, David's voice rang out, cutting through the noise, so that it stood out, singular and strong. "It's a story," David said, addressing Sarah and John, "about a man who tries to dig a hole so big that he can live beneath the surface of the Earth. On some days, he feels that he is above those who are far below him, on the other side of the world, but in the next instant, when he hears feet overhead, he feels that he is below those above him."

Sarah and John nodded in unison.

"He is always either far above or far below. He is afraid of the smooth, even surface."

"Ttttt," Harold snarled under his breath.

"Every encounter he has," David continued, "is

essentially his clunking up against this surface too eagerly, trying to burst through and ascend, but ricocheting off it and plummeting back down into the depths."

Harold half recalled a quote . . . He couldn't remember . . . He wanted to jump up now and dance his jig, but it wouldn't have the desired effect. The conversation had already moved on to something else; no one was looking at him. Harold wanted to get up and defend the character in the story David was describing—perhaps he was merely approaching things from an academic, and indeed a *literary* perspective—or perhaps the character was self-aware, and David didn't know what he was talking about!

Harold contracted his right bicep; his oxford button-up pulled taut against it; he did the same with his left. Harold flexed his quads, then biceps again. He wanted to eat. He wanted to go to the gym. Dolly's and David's voices swirled like a sewer drain behind Harold's close-set eyes. Harold breathed deeply twice, to bring himself back into his body. He tried to breathe into his thoughts.

And then he remembered the backpack. His shoulders tensed up, but when he looked down and saw it there, he relaxed. In the context of his colleagues, it had become almost a comforting presence: a secret hidden in plain sight, a special kind of knowledge that only he had access to. Plus, it might contain something that he could use to defend himself . . . The backpack gave him a feeling of control.

Dolly sat on the other side of the table, a few

chairs down. David laughed; it sounded like a novice trombonist practicing scales. Where was Casey? David—backpack—laughing—food. Why wouldn't anyone look at him? Harold felt like he was being squeezed. Shepherd sustains itself with squeezing, Harold thought. Shepherd College was not a college but a squeezing station, where everyone squeezed each other, and got squeezed by the college itself, and then drowned out the sounds of the squeezing with their academic work and explanations . . .

Harold sipped his water and flexed his biceps, trying not to scowl. He was strong, virile—yet here he was. This was the culmination of his entire life so far.

Harold had put his head down through undergrad, through his master's, through his PhD; he put his head down even now. Harold kept himself practically supine, curled up when touched, like a potato bug. But once he got tenure, he imagined, he'd unfurl himself. Harold would finally straighten his spine.

Casey had had tenure for as long as Harold had known him. Casey, like Harold, had kept his head down, but once Casey got tenure, nothing changed. "I thought getting tenure would set me free," Casey had told Harold one day over cold sandwiches, "but after I got tenure, I would sit down and write the same sentences I'd typed to get tenure, with one or two words changed." Casey's tone had become uncharacteristically confessional. "When I chose to go into academia, I'd felt disdain for academia," he'd said, "but I went into academia and, in the end, I became an academic."

Tenure didn't mean what it used to mean, he said.

Only the worst scum get tenure, he'd said, and tenure wasn't even tenure anymore—now they could still fire you at any moment.

The more the reality of Harold's situation revealed itself to him, the more depressed he became. Best-case scenario, he'd become complacent, teaching the same things year after year. Death continually renewed itself in the dead, as life did in the living. What characterized life was a process of *becoming*, of change. Harold could publish variations on the same themes he'd already written about, or develop some aspect of his last book more fully, but he could not meander into a new field of inquiry altogether. He didn't have the energy, or the capability, or the desire. His future seemed dim.

With tenure, the doom and self-loathing of tenure, Casey said, he'd been unable to sleep, unable to focus, unable to write or have any new thoughts. He would read the same few books over and over, understanding less and less, all the while getting more and more complacent. "If my satisfaction as a student and teacher were a graph," he'd said, "it would be an upside-down U shape, peaking at the moment I got tenure, then descending steeply from then on." The fact that Casey formulated his life as a graph set Harold's teeth on edge. "When I was young," Casey said, "I was full of life." He paused, assuming a strange face. "Now I am one of these micro men, framing life, like everything, neatly in a bleak graph, with no broad vision, no future or past." He'd said this in a faux-grandiose tone, like he was joking, but, as with all jokes, it concealed a brutal truth. This conversation had left Harold rattled, but not rattled enough to change. Harold still wanted tenure. If anything, he wanted tenure then more than ever. It was common for academics to disparage academia, Harold reasoned, especially when they had achieved success within it. Casey had tenure, and despite what he had said about it, it's not like he had rejected it. He clearly still wanted it, so Harold still wanted it too.

The fragmented nature of Harold's shrunken life depressed him. His colleagues' voices grew even louder, drowning out his thoughts, so that the voices seemed to *become* his thoughts. He imagined screaming; he "clicked" the air by opening and closing his throat with his mouth closed, almost like gulping, then coughed.

VIII

THE LAWES HALLS LED INCOHERENT BURSTS of marching students past their meeting room, which was not really a room but a crevice; a group of football players—who chided each other in boisterously thick and brassy tones—ambled past. Harold strained to hear their voices.

Harold imagined bigger versions of the kids he had grown up with: Chris, Duff, Jeff, Jaylen. As a child, Harold had excelled at sports. He excelled at physical activity in general—particularly tae kwon do, for which, when he was nine, Harold placed second in the national competition for *poomsae* (form) and third for sparring—but football didn't interest him. Even then, he'd felt it was too brutally team-oriented. Recently, however, Harold had begun to acquire an appreciation for it: many things that had formerly seemed arbitrary became meaningful after Harold started lifting weights. Despite all his mistakes that had caused him to drift further and further away from football—despite the way he'd lived his life until he started lifting weights—he was grateful that he could now engage with football in some way, by watching it or teaching the occasional player in class.

Out in the hall, one of the players yelled, then many laughed, and for a moment there seemed to be a pocket of genuine consensus in the building. Harold recalled a joke Casey had told him:

What is the only thing two academics can agree on?
How bad a third academic's work is.

The boisterous voices made Harold yearn for the gym. He wanted nothing more than to grip a barbell between his fingers and press up, to hear the clanging weights punctuated by the grunts of men: the brassy voices in the hall transformed into sounds of steel—clinking, crashing. He wanted to leave, to get up and go, now, but he still had a whole meeting to get through.

Suddenly, the door opened and a few students came in: muscled, fervent, loud; square jaws, open flannels with shirts or tank tops underneath, short shorts, backpacks.

Vance and Dolly sneered at them. Harold imagined Vance and Dolly as literal buzzards, flying around the room trying to peck the football players' eyes.

Professors and graduate students often complained that the college exploited them—it paid them very little for what amounted to a lot of work—but the college exploited football players most of all. The football team drew enormous crowds and brought in enormous sums of money, in addition to boosting morale. The players often practiced twice a day. They had to eat a certain way, and study plays in addition to schoolwork. During games, they faced immense pressure to win, and, on top of it all, they had to go to class and deal with the scornful abuse of their professors, which was perhaps the saddest aspect of their plight.

Literature professors hated football players, because football players worked harder than literature professors, and were smarter than literature professors. Football players engaged in an activity with stakes. Literature, on the other hand, was the domain of flounderers and bunglers, who, in the renowned Shepherd College, sought nothing other than protection from the consequences of their bungling. Literature was stale and obsolete, corrupted by a kind of bunglemania...

The professors hated the football players because they did not understand the football players, whereas the football players hated the professors because they understood them all too well. Harold had puzzled over this for years, observing with increasing interest that the enmity between the two groups seemed to grow exponentially, at least on the side of the professors—they were always complaining about how much funding was being allocated to sports-related things, whereas their departments were frequently getting their funding stripped—and

concluded that the thing that made the football players so resilient to the machinations of professors was
none other than their love of football: the football
players fought back against the deadening more than
any other student group on campus, essentially because they loved football. This love structured their
lives so that they regularly failed to do their home-
work, and this was in the end what saved them.

The intruding students, upon seeing that they'd
wandered into the wrong room, turned and left without saying a word.

Hey, Harold wanted to yell, wait up.

But then David approached him, with his hand
outstretched.

"Harold," David said. He gestured toward the
empty chair next to Harold, against which the backpack was leaning.

"Of course," Harold said, too distracted by the
presence of the backpack to come up with an excuse to
tell him not to sit there. Harold grabbed the backpack
and scooted it toward his chair, pushing it beneath the
table, between his legs. "How's it going?"

A grin broke out across David's face like acne.
His arm more closely resembled a spaghetti noodle
than an actual human arm. Harold took it and gently squeezed, nodding—although he was specifically
trying not to nod—jiggling David's whole arm up and
down. Harold felt as if he were flapping not a spaghetti
noodle but a pool noodle, slapping water, splashing
himself, uncomfortably wet. He resumed his position,
looking straight ahead.

As David lowered himself to sit, his frail legs wobbled and his big head bobbled atop his thin, dry neck. His scar crinkled.

"Sarah! John!" David cried. The names sprayed from his mouth. It was just like David, Harold thought, to call out to John and Sarah, just to prove that he was well liked in the department.

Harold hoped that one of them would respond, and perhaps even come over to engage David in a conversation until the meeting started. However, just as Harold had dreaded, and even predicted, but was ultimately unprepared for, David's mouth began to move.

"What?" Harold asked. He tried to focus his attention. "What?"

Harold could see the contours of David's lips as they stretched and contracted, making shapes, but he was unable to connect the shapes with any meaning.

Repulsed by David's thin lips and crumbly scar, he looked away. In the distance, Sarah and John slid their palms against each other's palms and clapped, mirroring each other's movements. There had recently been a "team building" seminar, during which, in addition to learning about inoffensive ways to discern what people felt comfortable talking about before asking any potentially insensitive questions (for example, instead of asking "How was your summer?," which could be traumatic if they'd visited their family, or had to work a second job, one might opt instead for something like "Are you comfortable talking about your summer?"), the keynote speaker also taught them games they could play to boost morale, essentially just various versions of "patty-cake."

Harold shuddered. He felt as if a thumb were pressing at the base of his throat. He did not go up and smack both of them in the face, as he wanted; rather, he sat there stupidly, with a tense jaw, in their little cramped room in the basement, trying to come up with something to say to David so that he wouldn't know that he hadn't been listening.

In a second or two, despite his inability to follow along as David spoke, Harold understood retroactively—as if part of his brain had unconsciously processed what was happening in real time, while another part produced a numb buzz that tried to suppress all understanding—what David had asked. Harold looked down at his phone, which he'd been gripping tightly in his clammy hand.

"Yeah," Harold said. "Only a few minutes past."

David's right ear twitched. His darting eyes made two quick flashes leftward. "Well. Glad to be back," he said, slapping Harold's back. "It was bitter cold in the Northeast this weekend. Bit-t-t . . ." David's head inched slightly toward Harold, as if he wanted to be petted.

David and some other faculty had traveled over the weekend to canvass for the socialist candidate—to "knock on doors," as some of the faculty had phrased it in the mass email, encouraging everyone to join them in their "fight against" various abstractions.

"Mm," Harold said, definitively.

This socialist candidate was, like all so-called American socialists, Harold thought, not actually a socialist but rather a socialist money-raiser, and, like all socialist money-raisers, he was guaranteed to lose. His only reason for running, it seemed, besides raising money, was to get David and other faculty to annoy Harold even more than they already did.

Harold's hand actually felt pulled toward David's head, but he resisted. The backpack seemed to shine in his periphery.

Just pet him, Harold thought.

On one hand, petting David might confound him to such a degree, and flood his mind with such a rush of endorphins, that any prior attention David may have paid to the backpack would surely vanish; on the other hand, such strange behavior on Harold's part might make David suspicious.

Even if David did notice, Harold thought, it's not like Harold was actually *wearing* the backpack—it was just near his feet. There was still some plausible deniability, even now.

Harold focused his eyes to see if he could discern the crosses on the zippers from where he sat. From a distance, they just looked like holes in the metal rectangles; David almost certainly couldn't see them.

"Sarah and John brought gloves, but I didn't even consider it, since we're in the South and mitten season is over..." David droned on about his trip, relaying anecdotes about Sarah and John and one particularly resistant "old geezer" who'd followed them shouting slurs until they were not only off his lawn but in their car, driving away.

Harold recalled an interaction he'd seen between

David and Casey online, which seemed to spring up from nowhere, blurring everything around it such that only the memory was sharp—but then the memory was gone, just as quickly as it came. Harold's jaw tightened. At any point, he thought, David could snap. David could say "Sarah and John" or "solidarity" or "election coming up" and snap. Or, I could snap first, Harold thought, with all the force and clarity of divine revelation. I could snap my jaw at David . . . and bite him! . . . Or perhaps I could just suck my teeth . . .

Harold turned his eyes in their sockets and watched David's leg bounce, mere inches from him, as he spoke. Couldn't David scoot over a little? There was more than enough room at the table, no reason for him to be wiggling and writhing like some kind of horny child, nearly rubbing up against me, sucking up all the oxygen, then breathing his hot, sour breath back out onto everyone . . .

Harold wanted to be at the gym.

He needed to lift.

I should quit my job and become a personal trainer, he thought. Perhaps if I become a personal trainer, I can undo some of this damage . . .

Harold imagined getting up, flicking David's head, and announcing, "I am going to become a personal trainer." He remembered a video in which a muscular boy in a weight belt walked through Barnes & Noble with a megaphone saying, "Fuck books. Books are for pussies. Go hit the gym."

David retrieved a coffee thermos from the outside pocket of his briefcase and slammed it down on the table, light glinting off the stainless steel, hurting Harold's eyes.

Harold reached down toward the backpack to finger the crosses.

Harold could pretend to be a Christian. The thought occurred to him with the instantaneous satisfaction of a joke. That would be another way to throw people off. The revelation of his having come to faith would distract even the most certain detectives: if it were possible for Harold to carry this cross backpack *because of the crosses*, then it was certainly possible for him to carry a backpack in general. As opposed to being the most damning aspect of the bag, perhaps it could be his strength.

No.

John and Sarah giggled in the distance, and Harold half expected them to fall down in a heap on the floor like children. Instead, they composed themselves after their outburst, like rubber rulers bent and then snapped back into place.

David had stopped talking about his trip; Harold, though maintaining an unrelated internal monologue, had managed to interject a few nods and noises of affirmation. Vance approached both of them and shook their hands. Harold looked up at Vance and accidentally smiled.

Vance said Harold's name in a vaguely official tone, and returned the smile warmly. For a brief moment, Harold thought he saw something flash in Vance's eyes, but when he blinked, it was gone. Vance's rosy, rotund face revealed nothing out of the ordinary.

It was not uncommon for scholars' physiognomy to reflect the work they taught, and Vance often behaved like a bashful yet chivalrous child from the Middle Ages, though he was a middle-aged man who had grown up in the 1980s.

Harold recalled the previous meeting, how Vance had stared at him, and the hallway earlier, where Vance had mocked his "snack stand." Harold had the impulse to avenge himself. He looked down at the backpack. "Take it," he said under his breath.

Vance looked at Harold, raising an eyebrow.

"I said take it," Harold said, "if you want it so bad."

But before Vance could reply, Dianthe entered the room, hips swaying, arms in the air, shaking her hands. "Hello," she said, drawing it out—"Helloooooo-ooohhh."

A few more shuffled in behind her, two of whom Harold didn't recognize, wearing frozen grins. Harold scanned the room for Casey.

IX

RUN, HAROLD THOUGHT. JUST RUN. HE IMAG-
ined picking up the backpack, then crashing through
the glass door in the hall, flying side-kicking it, shards
sticking in him—blood everywhere. He began map-
ping out the Lawes floor plan, trying to distract
himself from the swelling and contracting walls, his
chattering colleagues, their duplicitous tones. Perhaps
if he could inventory everything objectively, Lawes
would lose its power over him.

But just as Harold began to think about his surroundings—stairs—rubber edges—opening—halls—cluster
of classrooms—voices ricocheting off walls—glass door
leading to courtyard—offices—Harold's head prevented
him from visualizing a complete picture in his mind.

Run, Harold thought again, imagining himself
covered in glass.

Behind the main set of stairs was a hall, which led back toward a hidden stairwell, at the bottom of which was a broad platform. This was the only part of Lawes Harold could picture clearly. He had retreated into this stairwell many times, mainly to look at his phone. He wanted to go there now.

In this hidden stairwell, where he never saw anyone else, any slight noise—such as accidentally dropping one's keys or crinkling a receipt—echoed endlessly up, and each time Harold entered the stairwell, he imagined screaming "Help!"

Harold delighted in imagining the frightened expressions of those who might hear a scream coming up from nowhere underground.

One day, after having worked up the courage for months, Harold walked in and out of the stairwell three times; then, on the fourth, he screamed. The physical sensation of the scream—vibrating in his throat, tense muscles—was rapturous. He felt his voice in his chest. It felt good. Rapturous, Harold thought, then imagined that his scream actually foreshadowed the rapture, as if the echo ricocheting above him might create a spiral of sound that would then suck him up into it. Harold waited, crouched beneath the stairs, for someone to come rushing in to help whoever had let out such an agonized cry, but no one came. Harold imagined the sound of a creaking door and boots and heels; there was a crack, then whispering, feet shuffling—then nothing.

Harold's heart beat in the back of his neck. He leaned against the cold blue wall. His heart beat in the top of his head. His heart beat in his fingers. It was silent. Did his heartbeat make a sound, echoing up? He heard people now outside the stairwell. In his heightened state, he could hear even their sniffling. How could they not have heard his scream? Or his heartbeat? Or how could they have heard him and not cared?

The fluorescent lights had hissed and crackled, staticky, like dead air. Could the static buzz have drowned out his scream? After months of desire— months of *planning*, working up the courage—his great act had been met with total indifference. What had gone wrong?

Harold decided to give people the benefit of the doubt. So, shifting into a malevolent crouch, he inhaled deeply to generate power, and screamed again.

He let out a long, demented "rraaahhhhhhh," then added in three "ows," and even a "please, no," for good measure.

This time, there was not even a pant leg or a sneaker in the halls. There was only the lingering echo— diminishing with each passing second, until all that remained was a faint remnant, like a scent—then silence. Even the stairwell appeared farther away from him now, blurred, as if objects themselves were trying to escape him.

Nothing.

For the next week, between classes and meetings, Harold watched for those who regularly visited the area directly outside or above the stairwell around the time when he had screamed. He took notes in his phone: redhead, 5'3"; wavy hair, jaw; group, Asian.

His plan was to discern those who were likely to have heard it, and to simply ask them if they had heard anything strange. After this week of searching, Harold identified a few students who were there at the same time every day. Vance was also there some of the time. Harold spent days lurking around the stairwell, taking notes. He resolved to approach a student or two, but when the time came to confront them, he simply watched them pass.

One day, however, Harold was walking toward the stairwell and he bumped into a group of female students, two of whom he'd seen in the area with some regularity. As they were picking up the books that Harold had accidentally knocked to the ground, he decided to ask them if they'd heard anything.

"Have you," Harold began, then paused, seeing that they'd already begun to move away from him. "Hey." He addressed himself to no one in particular. "A couple days ago, or maybe a week, or—walking around this area . . . Did you hear . . . ?"

The students looked confused.

"If you could just try to think," Harold said, trying to put them at ease but accidentally sounding desperate, like he was pleading, and even grasping the air in front of him with his hands, as though trying to catch a bug, "it would help me a lot." He pulled his hands back into himself as he was overcome by an idea. "I'm a professor," Harold said. "I'm a professor and I'm conducting research." He laughed like a fork stabbing a chicken breast, then scraping the plate. "I want you guys to help me with my study."

The students shifted uneasily. Harold made his face appear thoughtful.

The tallest student in the group looked at her shoes.

"What study?" another student asked. "Wait. Are you an architecture professor?"

"An architecture professor? No," Harold said. "Are you sure you didn't . . ." he began, then stopped. "Why do you ask?"

The student appeared coy, as if she were hiding something. "No reason," the student said, grinning. "Listen, we have to go."

The girl who had been staring at her shoes now gawked at Harold with her mouth open. Did her face betray a knowledge of his scream? Harold tried to study her expression. He creased his eyes and wet his lips.

Students simply do not respect professors anymore, Harold thought. And, though that gaping, inscrutable face had consumed him for over a week, he soon forgot about the interaction. That is, until a month or so later, when he saw three men in neon vests holding a machine that looked like a metal detector up to the walls outside the hidden stairs. One of the workers had only one arm, which he used to hold the machine; there was a rounded stump at his shoulder where his other arm would have been, circling counterclockwise repeatedly, as if battery-powered.

"He is an architecture professor," Harold heard one of the workers say to the armless man. Harold tried to stand near enough to hear what else they were saying but far enough so that, were they to become aware of his presence, they wouldn't think he was intentionally eavesdropping. The way the worker had said "architecture professor" reminded Harold of the student; it wasn't a phrase he'd heard often—he'd gone whole years, it seemed, without hearing "architecture professor"—and to hear it twice so close together felt significant. Harold could make out certain words— "lunch," "bull"—but that was it.

It *was* around lunchtime that Harold had screamed at the base of the stairs, he thought, as he meandered around Lawes, feeling himself to be on the verge of some insight. Who knows what "bull" could have meant; perhaps they thought the sound came from a bull? What were they doing to the walls? What were they looking for? Harold stepped into one of the administrator's offices, intent on asking, but instead, seeing she wasn't there, he took a piece of candy off her desk.

Often, when Harold had a new idea, it came to him all at once and with astonishing conviction, then he worked the idea out over time, finding more evidence to support what had initially only been a glowing intuition. The idea presented itself in its entirety, then as he went about his life, the proof emerged. He would notice certain details he hadn't noticed before, and make connections between things that had previously seemed disparate and unrelated.

This was how his insight had emerged that fateful day, when he was blindsided by a question that would fundamentally change the way he thought about his job forever. *What if the men in neon vests were looking for the scream?*

What if, Harold thought, in the halls outside

those hidden stairs—the halls that enclosed them all like coffins—the building itself had sucked up his cry? What if his cry had been subsumed into a low-grade buzz, and this—not the fake light—was what he constantly heard?

For the first time in years he felt like he was on to something. So later that night, he investigated. Harold snuck into Lawes.

Not wanting to turn on any of the lights, potentially alerting anyone to his presence and ruining his experiment—it needed to be dark to test his theory—he felt his way along the walls with his right hand, holding his left arm out in front of him to feel for anything he might run into. It wasn't hard, upstairs, to find his way around, because some slivers of moonlight came in through the windows, but in the basement it was thickly dark. The dark felt like a substance he was stuck inside. The dark felt like a wall. Harold groped his way to the hidden stairwell, then sat, listening closely.

In the silence, alone, Harold tried to remain rational. There were no lights. There was no groaning heater or air conditioner. There were no students or colleagues or administrators talking, no laptops or projectors being used. Yet Harold could still hear the steady buzz.

He ran through a list in his head: beehives in the wall; something vague about "the frequency of the Earth"; some kind of feedback from an amplifier? Nothing made sense. Then, just at the moment when Harold felt most despairing, on the verge of leaving and forgetting about his experiment altogether—maybe

even of quitting his job and becoming a hermit—
Harold received a gift: suddenly, he was soaring far
above his colleagues, looking down on them. He sat
up straight with his shoulders back.

In an empty or otherwise quiet college, Harold
thought, imagining himself giving a speech in front of
his colleagues, one can always hear a steady buzz. Harold imagined his colleagues' expressions. He would lay
out his revelation just this way. He would lull them
into a state of deceptive comfort—then lift the knife.

In an empty or otherwise quiet college, Harold
thought, sitting there in the dark, one can always hear
a steady buzz; and this steady buzz is often attributed
to the air-conditioning or fluorescent lights, but this
is a mistake: the sound is actually always there. It is—
Harold paused dramatically—*coming from the walls.*
Shivering now in the black hall, Harold ran through
the possibilities again. No students, no teachers, no
AC, no light. The only thing left, Harold paused, was
his scream. No one had heard his scream because the
walls had sucked it up! This was Harold's insight, which
he would announce in his speech to his colleagues: the
walls had sucked up not only his scream but all such
screams since the founding of the school, such that the
low-grade hissing and flickering buzz was in reality one
single sustained cry, made up of the countless individual cries that had been sucked up by the floors and walls
and ceilings of Shepherd College since its beginning.

After that night, Harold had conducted more
research—he tried to record the sound on his phone; he
began watching ghost hunter videos on YouTube; he'd

occasionally ask Casey or Dolly, "Did you hear that?"—and his private revelation only grew. He searched every academic database for "scream" + "university"; "cries" + "walls"; he read the results and pieced together what he could. Of course, nothing he found stated anything explicitly; but through a combination of close and far reading, creative thinking and freewriting—applying every mode of intellectual investigation he had learned and taught so far—he formed a better picture in his head of how things worked.

The college had sucked up cries of innocent victims going back to the school's founding—and you could hear it when you removed the academic explanations.

SITTING IN THE meeting room, Harold closed his eyes and focused. Beneath his colleagues' voices he could hear it. Beneath the tinny stress of Vance's voice, Dianthe's soothing boom, Dolly's lilting drawl, and David's clicking teeth, Harold could hear the hidden cries. They were crying out to him specifically. They were trying to tell him something. The walls were breathing. They were leaking. The walls were leaking into his head. Harold looked up at where the ceiling met the wall—where the white met white was a slightly yellow white, like someone had used plaster, or painted along the corner—and, descending into his seat, like a spiral sucking him into himself, he recalled the white tiles of the ceiling of his childhood basement again.

Vance announced that today Sarah would be taking minutes—a different tenured member of the faculty transcribed each meeting, in alphabetical order—then they took a vote to approve the previous meeting's minutes. After everything had been approved, hands raising in unison, Vance moved on to announcements. "The dean has informed me that they are planning to announce which departments will be given permission to hire for the next calendar year by the end of the semester. I hope we all—"

The white-on-slightly-yellow-white corner seemed to seep through Harold's eyes and down into his gut, where the past lived. There in his chair, as Vance droned on, Harold became a child again, remembering the corner where the wall met the ceiling in his childhood basement.

When Harold was a child, he hid things in the basement ceiling tiles, for no other purpose than to have a little secret, the thrill of which would fill him when he'd check in on his objects. Harold would grab one of his parents' green folding chairs, stack a box or a pile of folded towels on it so that he could reach, then hoist himself up, pushing his chosen tile up and peeking in on his hidden treasure: a Pop-Tart wrapper, a broken action figure, a pen. The hidden objects made him feel charged and alive. He would stare at them, afraid to touch or move them, then he'd carefully set the tile down.

The basement of that house had seemed, if not imbued with special capabilities, at least a place where special things occurred. This was in part due to its ambiguity of purpose: Harold had never quite understood what the basement was "for." And after Harold's family moved when he was twelve, his memories of that first basement overtook his recollections of that house as a whole, such that, after a time, he felt as if he'd never been anywhere else as a child, the basement constituting the sole landscape of his memories.

Harold's father's modest home gym was in that basement, but for most of Harold's childhood the fact of the home gym eluded him: a strange, labyrinthian pulley system, with a weight set next to it—all of which his eyes simply grazed over. He passed the gym hurriedly when he went to check in on his ceiling objects or fling his tiny body onto the couch at the other end of the room to watch TV. The cables and bars of the home gym appeared like creeping black vines, or cursive letters on a page.

One aspect of the gym area that Harold did like was the mirror: Harold's dad had a floor-to-ceiling mirror that took up the whole wall in front of the weights, and Harold would stare at himself for long stretches of time, sometimes for so long that his face began to split in two, or his eyes would become one eye—then snap back into two again.

When Harold turned twelve, his father tried to teach him how to use the weights, and Harold often recalled, on days like today—chest and tricep day—the time his father tried to teach him how to do a tricep pushdown. "Push down," Harold's dad had said, placing his hand on Harold's tricep, "and squeeze," but Harold wasn't able to squeeze. He tried a few times, then gave up.

The slightly less white paint in the corner of the

ceiling perturbed Harold now—why hadn't they painted it the same shade as the ceiling?

The undergraduate committee was updating everyone on the new introductory course to the major, which they'd been working on for nearly two years, and about which, Kirk said, "a consensus was now forming" among them, finally.

Harold's eyes found their way back to the corner, since they had nowhere else to go, and through a series of unconscious maneuvers, he was standing in his childhood basement, playing out his only recurring nightmare as a child.

The nightmare entered Harold through the corner where the ceiling met the wall, as a daydream, and Harold descended into the past, the basement materializing as a dream in his memory, until there was some commotion in the meeting room—another of his colleagues came in late—and so Harold's mind was fractured, split between two rooms: the meeting room and his childhood basement. Harold's eyes swiveled to see Frank—a frail, sullen professor of East Asian literature, who had dark bags under his eyes, and a hunchback—enter and sit, but in his mind he saw his father on one of the dark green folding chairs his family kept in the unfinished back room, "the dirty room." His father momentarily took on a Frank-like demeanor, and wore a purple tie, like Frank. Then Harold closed his eyes to try to free himself of Frank. He tried to focus, but he had become too self-aware, his memory had become too effortful, so that instead of occurring from his first-person point of view—seeing his father transform into an oily, roaring obstacle; jaw unhinged, wide; mouth swallowing his face—Harold saw himself as a child standing there, watching himself while his monster-father howled stretched-out vowel sounds and similar creatures burst through the ceiling and bathroom and back room, writhing and reaching toward him, until child-Harold was crying, trying to hide behind the weights.

The nightmare had felt like prophecy. It happened in the same way every time, but whenever Harold woke, the terror it inspired felt new; however, its power remained only for a moment as he peeled back the covers, sticky with sweat, and was soon forgotten, as the concerns of the day made themselves manifest—Harold peed, showered, got dressed, ate—then reoccurred in his mind occasionally in the following decades, as it did now.

Frank, despite coming in late, reminded everyone that the theme for the undergraduate literary contest this year was "First Words," and to hand out the new flyers, as well as remind the students about the contest again, because the year prior only three people had submitted, and so they had to award the prizes to those three by default.

"The Larmey family deserves better," he said solemnly. Frank adjusted himself. "This year, the Larmeys also suggested the theme, because Mrs. Larmey said that Jonathan's first word was when his love of literature began."

Jonathan Larmey was the student who'd been stabbed to death on campus three years before. He

was an English major, and his family created this undergraduate literary prize in his honor, to encourage
young writers to pursue their passions, since Jonathan
was robbed of his chance. "I tried to send an email to
you guys to get your thoughts," Frank said, "but maybe
you didn't see it . . . So I told her the theme was okay.
In the meantime, I found this quote." Frank pulled his
phone out of his pocket and fumbled with it. "Ah, er,
never mind"—he put his phone away—"but basically
it's just about how every writer becomes a writer because they had a formative experience with words, or
the power of words."

Occasionally, a person's thoughts harmonize with
something outside of them to such a degree that the
internal and external worlds feel mysteriously merged;
the distance between them seems so small that they
are lying flat on top of one another; and in this instance, Harold dimly sensed that his reflecting on his
childhood had somehow *caused* Frank to bring up the
Larmey Prize; it had even reached back into the past
and chosen this theme, "First Words." Harold's ear-
liest memory, for most of his life, was of being with
his mother and his younger brother in the basement
and there saying his first word: "skateboard." What
were the chances that this meeting would get switched
last-minute to this basement room in Lawes, where
the white-on-white corner was just like the white-
on-white corner in Harold's childhood basement?
And what were the chances that in the exact moment
Harold was transported back into that basement (or
the exact moment that his childhood basement had

reached forward into the basement room in Lawes), Frank would burst into the room, only to inform them all of the Larmey Prize's theme?

Until Harold was in his mid-twenties, he had a vivid memory of saying "skateboard" to his mom. He also remembered his mom *telling him* that his first word was "skateboard." But it wasn't until he was an adult, when he and his mom were reminiscing about how his father had ripped up the basement carpet one winter so that Harold and his brother could skateboard on the cement underneath, when Harold mentioned that he "couldn't believe how cool" it was that his first word had been "skateboard," that his mom had looked at him uneasily. "Uh-huh," she said, half smiling.

"What?" Harold asked.

"Very funny." His mom laughed. "You know your first word was 'mom.' '*Ma*.'"

Each of them thought the other was joking.

"How could your first word be 'skateboard'?" his mom said. "That wouldn't even make sense."

That night, Harold had a hard time looking at himself in the mirror. The "skateboard" memory had been an integral part of Harold's sense of self; it had made him feel mature and unique—similar to his "disproving the existence of Santa" to his mom when he was four—and after this new knowledge, Harold was filled with bitter shame. To whom had he told this "skateboard"-as-first-word story? Had anyone believed him? In retrospect, it was ridiculous.

Harold had been a fat, happy baby but a frail and

miserable kid. Growing up, he didn't have many close friends and had always felt that his peers understood something about how to live that he had never learned. At Harold's first sleepover, he had stayed up all night, eyes squeezed shut, only pretending to sleep, terrified that the other kids were playing a prank on him, that at any moment they would get up and leave him all alone. He overcompensated for this feeling by retreating deeper into himself, and there nurturing a sense of superiority—he rose in his mind, but he shrank from the world—until he turned out to be good at skateboarding.

Skateboarding, that physical activity that had seemed like any other physical activity, had in reality led Harold to quit all other forms of *structured* physical activity, like sports, before ultimately quitting even skateboarding itself—abandoning everything physical for the pursuit of pure language—and left him, in one final act of deception, with the false memory of his first word: "skateboard."

Sitting in the meeting room, Harold experienced a nauseating claustrophobia: the solid ceiling seemed to creep down, descending until it hovered just above his head, everything spinning, past and present conspiring to crush him in his chair. Ripped-up carpet—convoluted halls; his torso and neck were being pressed from within.

Harold felt clammy and wet, although his skin was abnormally dry.

He looked at David, then the backpack.

Harold needed to move his body. He needed to

do push-ups. His body inched upward, as if to stand, but his momentum was destroyed by indecision: he couldn't do them in the bathroom stall, or around any of the urinals, because his face would invariably hover inches away from pee that had "missed," and he couldn't do them near the sinks because he'd be too exposed—he wouldn't have time to jump up if anyone entered.

Dolly asked Kirk what was going on with the implementation of the new Gen Ed requirements, how they were affecting enrollment . . .

Kirk started to say something as Harold took out his phone, then put it away, not consciously processing anything; he took out his phone again, navigated to his Notes app—holding his phone next to his leg to conceal it from others' view—then exited Notes app and put his phone away.

"Dead on," Kirk said enthusiastically to something Dolly said, which Harold had missed.

Kirk always used the phrase "dead on" . . . Dead on, Harold thought, mocking Kirk's tone. He remembered when Kirk had recently quoted Paul de Man in a conversation with him . . .

Linguistic, he thought, distractedly . . . Lingui . . .

"Dead on" . . .

Words floated around Harold's head like blimps, bumping into one another, then drifting slowly into the distance.

Language was a kind of death, Harold thought, but death wasn't made of language. Or was it? Whenever Harold focused for too long on a sentence, or read for an extended period, he felt dead. In some sense, he *was* dead. He disappeared into another consciousness and, for a time, Harold ceased to exist. Reading required that the reader die. Harold had tried to stay alive while reading and couldn't. He tried to think and read at the same time—but he could only read and then think, or think and then read, and never the two simultaneously. In order to read, Harold had to disappear; after reading, it always took Harold a moment to come back to himself. At Shepherd, Harold was surrounded by death. Perhaps language itself *was death*, and was inherently at odds with life.

Thinking again of the undergraduate writing contest, and glancing up at the white-on-white corner, Harold tried to trace his descent.

Harold's formative experiences, and many of his subsequent experiences, consisted of words' slippery, malevolent art. This was in part what attracted him to literature: one could construct a new world, and nestle himself there within it. As a kid, Harold would lie, then get caught in the lie, then continue the lie. His pride led him to humiliation, but once he found himself there, he would humiliate himself even more.

So, Harold wrote sentence after sentence. These sentences were not just words or combinations of words that might as well be true, or that he could use indiscriminately to his middlingly nefarious ends, or to no clear end other than his own small pleasure: they were invisible corners and walls; giant, hollow tunnels and shoots, which made small rooms, deflecting and directing all potential futures into one—a future effortfully corrupted by signs and symbols and a perversion of will. Harold's life became more chaotic as he learned more words. This was proof as good as any that words had had a bad effect on him. Words, in the end, had ruined his life. They had taken the future and crammed it into the sickly fists of consciously articulated thought.

Words, like light through water, Harold thought—remembering something he'd read—only refracted that which they were meant to represent. Words did not interpret and convey but rather sucked up and mangled; and in the end, they not only sucked up and mangled but utterly and unequivocally annihilated. This was, Harold suspected, what had initially attracted him to literature: an unyielding need to destroy.

More than his wasted youth, and his low-paying career, this was the true tragedy of Harold's existence as an academic: he had dedicated his life to the transmission of acidic fluids that corroded everything they touched. Harold was an acidic fluid hawker, plain and simple. With each lesson, despite his best efforts to say true or, at least, "generative" things that would enrich or at least "stimulate" his students, Harold hawked acidic fluid at them, fat green loogies that burned their eyes and corroded their skin—and then worked their way inward.

Of course, Harold did not see the green slime that flung from his mouth and then sizzled and dripped on their faces and arms: he only saw its effects. When Harold would have the same student in class more than once over the course of four years, it was invariably the case that by the time he had them again, their face would have decayed: those who had been beautiful and vibrant at the beginning of the semester would have developed acne or wrinkles or sagging skin beneath their dimming eyes; some would have gained so much weight that Harold no longer recognized them; some would have gotten much thinner, their skin drooping down over their bones; some began to look as if their faces had been smudged with an eraser.

This was all, of course, Harold thought, because of the effects of words on still-developing brains. These words, which the students encountered in no structured way whatsoever, having no foundation to prepare them, parasitized the students like leeches. Language sucked up and destroyed his students, in the same way it had sucked up and destroyed Harold in his youth. Harold's students' decay was the result of being *taught*. Harold entered the classroom and, despite his efforts to the contrary, taught them imperceptibly.

"Such is the case with language, not least *our* language, that degraded hodgepodge of only the most nonsensical aspects of the most disparate languages," Casey once told Harold, when Harold had confided in him about his acidic fluid hawking. "However," he continued, "even if we did speak a beautiful language like French, or wrote in a beautiful language like Arabic, or even had an effective language—if such a thing existed—it would not make the slightest difference, and, in the end," he said, "we would use our language to pervert and destroy, just as the French have used their language to pervert and destroy, and the Arabs have used their languages to pervert and destroy, and everyone through all time has used their language to pervert and destroy."

They had been sitting on a bench, drinking coffee, shortly after Harold had begun to suspect something had gone horribly wrong in his life. He felt weak and ineffectual, confused and sick; and Casey had seemed like a beacon of hope in the dim college. Casey was tenured and strong and seemed contented. Harold looked up to him; everyone did. He was a model for Harold, as he was for a lot of the faculty, although in different ways for each of them.

"Words," Casey had said, "are parasites of reality, which have become so engorged with reality's blood so as to seem, to that ugly French nothing-master"—he grinned—"like *the only real thing*, but they are nothing more than a mirage. This is the great irony of the Frenchmen our colleagues fawn over," he'd said. "Just like the Christians, the Frenchmen emphasize The Word, but their conception of The Word is just a system of symbols and signs, signifying and referencing only each other, whereas for Christians The Word is not a word at all, but the truth—a person. It's a person and a *relationship*. These nothing-masters, who are really truth-rejectors, and therefore person-deniers, are, like the words they give ultimacy to, parasites."

"We're working on admissions," David said, during the graduate school report. "We got permission from the dean to make our offers. We've made five for master's, three for PhD, but we're still waiting to hear back."

Harold looked up and around, scanning his colleagues' faces for Casey, then he glanced down at the backpack between his legs.

David's arms rose slightly, then went limp.

"There is no word that can be uttered, written, or produced in the academy of the twenty-first century that can describe or communicate reality," Casey had said at the end of their long conversation on the bench, "because there are no major figures in the academy of the twenty-first century with muscles."

Harold couldn't tell if he was kidding.

"They talk about bodies," Casey continued, in his self-assured way, "but they don't mean bodies. They mean words. Look at their bodies. They look like words. There is no better defense against the parasitic nature of language than to have a strong body. The academy is infested with vampires," Casey was ranting, "who have become so lopsided by their focus on words that their very existence has come to mirror that of words: constantly typing and deleting and editing. They are, in effect, writing and reading themselves. Academics have ceased to look or act like people, and they've begun to look and act like words; not even full sentences, or paragraphs—but individual words. Being in full flight from reality and descending at an unprecedented rate into madness, they spend their time diddling their too-thick or too-thin thumbs, wringing their soft hands over nothing and pretending to be wringing their soft hands over everything, saying things like 'It isn't even obvious that the *self*, as such, exists' or '*Reality* and *truth* and *beauty* are only sinister tools of disguised ideology' or 'Everyone is equal and the same in every way,' and all of this is the result of not having a body. Academics are not people but word-people; not word-people but words! In short, they have become what they think the universe is made of—the printed word; that is to say dead matter."

The next morning, Harold bumped into Casey in the hall. He turned and walked with Casey in the opposite direction to where he'd been going, and when they stopped in front of Casey's classroom, Harold asked Casey to take him to the gym.

X

DURING "NEW BUSINESS," SARAH STAMMERED
her way through some logistics. Harold could just
make out the gist through all of her self-interruptions
and meandering sentences: the Office of Development
had asked the department to create a list of "departmental priorities," something related to fundraising.

Sarah was obviously once very pretty, Harold reflected, but her face had become scrunched over the
years. There were multiple ripples on her forehead,
and her jowls, though taut against her rigid jaw, still
somehow gave the impression of bloat. Sarah was always with John, who kept nodding and biting his lip as
she spoke, and she had even started dressing like John;
John was also always with Sarah, and in fact had started
dressing like Sarah. Harold looked back and forth between them, and each time he noticed something new

they both shared: Sarah wore a yellow blouse, John wore yellow socks; Sarah wore a brown clip in her hair, John wore brown slacks. Whereas before, one could recognize John instantly from a distance, because he almost exclusively wore bright yellow T-shirts with the covers of novels on them, now, if one saw bright yellow materializing in the distance, like a school bus, it could be one of Sarah's new blouses or coats.

Though young, John was preternaturally adept at navigating departmental politics, shape-shifting and changing to rise in both esteem and rank, like a lawyer in a law firm, except less straightforwardly aggressive, whereas Sarah was neurotic, obsessed with politics, severe. In addition to their dress, Sarah and John imitated these qualities in one another. However, they both failed to truly embody these qualities, so they ended up infusing their original ugliness with less-integrated ugliness, copied from each other. Sarah infused her neuroticism with careerist ambition, whereas John infused his careerist ambition with neuroticism.

Harold, growing weary, looked down at the backpack; his vision blurred; shoulders and heads in his periphery lost their definition and became floating orbs; the walls appeared pixelated; everything turned vaguely reddish purple again. Harold was a loose tooth in the mouth of a suffocating face. Harold's body felt desiccated, shell-like, stomach rumbling—he was all stomach—as the blathering of neurotics cut like pins inside his ears. The present was a particled, crystalline shard, stabbing the past and future simultaneously and breaking Harold into pieces.

A debate had begun about a new lecture series. Some felt that more funding was needed, especially because of the high speakers' fees—the speaker coming next week would be paid $15,000—and others felt the money could be better spent elsewhere. They needed to hire a new creative writing professor; the discipline had been growing at an unprecedented rate, and class sizes were exceeding what the creative writing professors felt was feasible, or useful, for a workshop setting. Literature classes meanwhile were shrinking, and Harold easily understood why.

They also needed more people to teach in the writing center. The graduate programs had decreased enrollment, because there weren't many jobs for the students when they graduated, and it was unethical to let people dump years of their life into a degree they couldn't use, but this meant that the writing center was understaffed.

Harold squeezed the backpack between his feet, keeping himself entertained by applying different amounts of pressure and seeing how the bag responded.

It went on like this until heads started nodding, arms rising like weeds sprouting up through concrete. Harold lifted his too, despite not knowing what they were voting on, because going with the consensus would make the meeting go faster, and even this slight movement might be good for his muscles. He began piecing together what had happened from the fragments of conversation he now heard.

Dianthe and Dolly, he'd gleaned, were going to send out an email to the creative writing students telling them that the talk taking place in four weeks, which was to be given by an author Casey had invited, was no longer mandatory, due to some remarks the author had made in a recent interview that were not sufficiently disapproving of the president.

Harold disagreed with their reasoning, but he supported his colleagues' decision to make the talk optional. Readings and talks were always disastrous, even when they were given by brilliant authors, because even the most brilliant authors found themselves floundering when forced to explain themselves. When an author is asked about something he has written, or forced out of some necessity to give some sort of "talk," it is always and in every case abominable. Talks are manufactured out of thin air, for the sole purpose of money or getting pats on the head, and these manufactured-out-of-thin-air talks are never beneficial for the audience in any way. Someone manufactures a talk out of thin air, in order to get a pat on the head, ostensibly to give the audience something of value, but if one listens closely, nothing the speaker says makes sense at all. However, the audience never listens closely, because they're also there only to get pats on the head—pats of a lesser and more contemptible sort—which is why the only thing more reprehensible than a manufactured-out-of-thin-air talk is the audience that attends it. The audience listens, or pretends to listen, in many cases just salivating to ask a question, pointed at the speaker—who is really a jester—like a knife, masking their true intention behind a false one. A question-asker at a "talk" foists himself upon some subject he has no business with; he has traveled, like someone possessed, to a manufactured-out-of-thin-air talk, only to sit patiently as he is brutalized by some bungler who is only trying to get patted on the head, and then asks a question that is really just a comment, often in a completely unseemly manner that is impossible to follow. In short, Harold agreed with the decision to make the talk optional, because the students would get nothing out of it anyway.

Harold hadn't spoken the whole meeting, and now, in an attempt at a joke, he asked whether the talk would be optional for faculty too.

No one responded, or even smiled. Harold clenched and unclenched his glutes three times in quick succession, then squeezed them until they burned.

This is how they treat him when he tries to say something good-natured? Did they not hear him?

The faculty . . . Harold thought, then had a breakthrough: Faculty—they were a cult . . . They were—

"And now, the last topic of discussion," Dolly looked in Harold's direction, as if to underscore her seriousness, "we have our very special speaker coming next week for this Friday's colloquium."

Harold had totally forgotten about the colloquium. This, he knew, was mandatory. At least, unofficially. Anyone who didn't show would be under suspicion. He touched the backpack.

Dolly, speaking for all of them, said she knew that they "were all really looking forward to this," and that she was "eager to get a fresh perspective" on how the faculty could "better serve our Shepherd community,

especially with everything that's happened recently."
Her voice was different now; her accent had disappeared, and she wasn't adding "oh" to the ends of
words randomly. She sounded like a mother repri-
manding her child in public—urgent, hushed, masking shame. She flipped her hair and twisted up her lips.
"It will be followed by drinks at Milkboy for all who
care to join."

Milkboy, Harold thought, mimicking her tone—
how demoralizing. There were never any drinks at
Milkboy, only weapons of brutality, he thought. Another blunt object, with spikes in certain places . . .

"In light of recent events," Dolly's voice droned on.

Everyone, including Harold, nodded, murmuring
vague affirmations. He could feel the acid eating away
at his stomach lining.

Harold was starving. His muscles were atrophying.
He tried not to nod, but his head continued to nod,
and an agreeable noise came from his mouth.

Harold wasn't sure which recent events Dolly
meant. Everything the department did now was "in
light of recent events," as if they were all hooked up to
an "in light of recent events" machine that caused them
to react, not only alone but "as a department," to every recent event, endlessly. English departments were
no longer, strictly speaking, English departments but
rather recent event departments, where "recent events,"
and not literature, were the prism through which everything was read.

Harold gripped the backpack in his feet and
squinted. The crust around the lid of David's thermos

looked weeks old; the fluorescent light glinted off the silver; the thermos appeared egregiously tubular. Harold curled his left arm slightly and squeezed. He did it again, focusing on the bicep, moving his arm slowly, balling his fist. All at once, the room was silent. Everyone was looking at him.

Could they have caught him flexing? Harold had only lifted his arm a little—but still, he'd flexed and they all turned simultaneously, at the exact moment . . . Was it the backpack? No. A thought that usually disturbed him now calmed him: Harold wasn't able to contract his left arm that well. Harold had always had a harder time contracting his left bicep than his right, and so sometimes he practiced contracting the muscle by subtly training it throughout the day. However, even when he was practicing, he most often could only consciously contract the muscle weakly—it barely moved—so, in this instance, despite his initial fear, it was unlikely that anyone would have actually seen his left arm flex any more than it naturally did when he moved his arm in general.

Harold tried to replay the fragments he'd registered of what Dolly had said. Did someone ask him a question? Was this the moment he'd finally get accused of harboring some secret?

"Casey," Vance said, in a friendly tone. "You know how to set it up?" Vance stared straight at Harold and gestured toward the overhead projector.

Harold looked into Vance's eyes, planning to hold them, in front of everyone, now that Vance had misspoken and accidentally called Harold by the wrong name—Harold would pretend he didn't realize the mistake and let Vance simmer in his awkward defeat—but Vance would not lock eyes with Harold. Vance appeared to be staring at Harold's forehead, or his hair. I know what you're up to, Harold thought, you little twerp. You act all high and mighty when it's just us and the "snack stand," but when the pressure's on and the whole department is watching you crack—you look past me instead of at me. You misspeak because you know that I will crush you, here and now.

Aha! Harold knew how to win. He twisted his neck around like a wrung towel—but behind Harold, where Vance was looking, Frank sat in a neon green plastic chair.

"Sorry," Vance said, turning red. "Frank."

Frank made his way to the front of the room. Harold imagined Frank as Casey, and the image reminded Harold of a well-proportioned horse: his broad shoulders and strong arms in his tucked-in button-up; his glutes, round and firm in his slacks. Of everyone he worked with, even the women, Casey had the most succulent glutes; Frank had no discernable glute muscles, his butt appeared flat as a laptop screen in his dark slacks. Harold leaned forward a little, contracting his own.

"Is there a way to connect my laptop?" John asked, also walking to the front. John looked horrible. His eyes flitted back and forth between Frank and the computer. "My students always help with the technology," he said. "It makes me feel so old." This got an approving laugh from many of the faculty—of whom John was the youngest.

Frank asked John what he was trying to do. "It's a graphic from a friend at NYU," he said. "I have everything online, in my email. Email is online, right?"

This got fewer laughs than before, partly because people had stopped paying attention. At Shepherd College, one had to constantly engage the faculty with some trifle, usually a piece of gossip or something they could use as gossip later, or they'd be lost in an instant.

Frank turned on the computer, then the projector.

The computer was on a podium on the right side of the room. John pressed himself against the wall and slithered along it, in an attempt to make space for Frank to pass, but he moved too quickly, and inadvertently boxed Frank in. They did a kind of dance; Frank broke free.

Harold had always thought of John as small, and he was small, but Harold noticed as he wiggled back and forth and sort of hopped and shimmied in front of Frank that he had a little gut. Casey and Harold had a nickname for him, John Von Winklestein.

Whenever John got excited, he involuntarily winked. John said *Terry Eagleton* and winked. John said *Walter Benjamin* and winked. John said *Michel Foucault* and *Berthold Brecht* and *capital* and winked. John said *ideological* and *ideologies* and *power* and *access to power* and *there is no reason why* . . . all the while taking an unseemly pleasure . . . Something stirring . . . An indecent delight.

Harold contracted his glutes again, this time peering furtively at David. Harold's muscles tingled and his body raised up slightly as his flaccid butt hardened into something thick and firm. Harold relaxed. He sank back down.

Then he became aware of his hip flexors. His hip flexors were surely shrinking, since his legs had been bent at a roughly ninety-degree angle for such a long stretch of time. He needed to stand and elongate them. His shoulders were hunched too—his posture was terrible—he needed to stretch. He needed to straighten up, now.

When one's hip flexors get shorter from sitting, it causes "anterior pelvic tilt," in which the hips point down, the lower back curves, and the belly protrudes. Rounded shoulders, on the other hand, cause a hunched upper back, which, in turn, makes one's chest smaller, because the rounded shoulders decrease the surface area of the pectoral muscle. Harold felt his body slowly morphing into this unnatural shape. Harold had recently tested his posture, by standing straight up and letting his hands fall to his sides: his thumbs, he saw, were pointed toward each other, whereas ideally, he'd learned from a YouTube video, one's thumbs should point straight ahead. Harold hated his hunched posture, because it was the posture of the masses; Harold was an exceptional man—he straightened up.

As Harold straightened up, his right hip flexor vibrated for a decisecond, as if his body were rebelling, or reminding him again of its existence. The body had a language one could learn, he thought, unlike the language of his colleagues, who . . . He felt his hip flexor again—ffff.

Harold took out his phone and texted Casey: "The Winker is preparing a powerpoint. Where are you?"

Harold grinned, holding his phone next to his leg.

Harold stared at John for a reaction, but John was looking at Frank. Usually, when Casey and Harold texted during meetings, they would sneak mischievous glances and grin, but now Casey seemed to be avoiding him—he wasn't even there. Harold felt a pang of paranoia—their texts and interactions had seemed normal lately. Where was he?

What if Casey had seen him earlier, and noticed the backpack? When was the last time they actually spent quality time together? Harold quickly tried to think of the last time they'd hung out, but he abandoned the thought. Harold considered texting again, to gauge his reaction, but stopped himself. Was Casey somehow his enemy now?

"One second . . ." John said. "I'm . . ."

Harold felt unwell. He was hungry. And the backpack . . . Even in the worst-case scenario, Harold thought, Casey would understand. If there was anyone Harold could trust completely at Shepherd College, it was Casey.

Ben, who taught American literature, and who for some reason had braces, was sitting by himself in a corner. He looked like he had a giant, invisible structure stuck between his skull and his skin, which made his face strangely contort. His thin lips were stretched at an unsightly angle, gums showing. His mouth seemed to take up his entire face. His eyes were small and crooked. His nose was small. His cheeks were tight, but there were still little chunks that hung loosely. He was constantly sniffling and making slurping sounds. Slightly in front of Ben, Yi sat staring straight ahead like a brick.

"Aha," John said, sounding simultaneously nervous and relieved. He adjusted his posture, exhaled audibly, then began speaking an octave or two higher than he'd been speaking before. "So," he began, "in light of every-thing that's been going on"—John's pointer and middle fingers repeatedly made the "scissor cutting" motion by his sides—"I thought I'd share this graphic, which I found super helpful, and which I thought we could all spend some time thinking about this week, in advance of the visit from our very special guest. As educators, I think we'd all agree that it's important for us to stay vigilant, and to remain students ourselves . . ."

Harold's headache returned as he began to dread how hungry he'd be once he got to the gym. His shrunken stomach seemed to rise into his mouth. Maybe he could stop at 7-Eleven, get a protein bar, and do some grading in the car while it digested?

Harold refocused his eyes on the screen: a list of fourteen words, with bubbles branching off each, con-taining definitions.

1. *Perfectionism*
2. Sense of Urgency
3. Defensiveness
4. Quantity over Quality
5. Worship of the Written Word
6. *Only One Right Way*

7. *Paternalism*
8. Either/or Thinking
9. Power Hoarding
10. Fear of Open Conflict
11. Individualism
12. Progress Is Bigger, More
13. Objectivity
14. *Right to Comfort*

The image was pixelated; the text that branched off the giant words was tiny. John, presumably seeing all the squinting eyes, offered to read it aloud.

"While some of these might seem startling," he said, his voice blending with the walls and the ceiling, such that Harold had to search it out intentionally, "... how these ideas work to create a kind of implicit ideological hegemony ..." Harold's heart rate increased—when John said the word "hegemony" his right eye slapped closed; Harold could hear the lids wetly squish, like a quarter dropped in water, or a stepped-on bug. "We are haunted by our collective past," he said. "It's important that we look at our demons—that we conjure demons, so to speak—in order to learn."

Harold squinted to read the text next to "5. Worship of the Written Word."

"This idea prioritizes documentation and writing skills, as opposed to the 'ability to relate with others.' It also leads to teaching that there is 'only one right way' to do something."

Harold felt defensive, which was, he grimly realized, word number three on the screen.

The flat, tiled floor felt sharp beneath his shoes. His feet tingled. Harold needed to stomp them, but he did not want to cause a scene, so he stomped them imperceptibly... Hear my stomp! he mouthed—but they could not hear his stomping. Only he knew what was really going on. He understood something that belonged to him alone—*my stomps!* he thought. The sounds around him now were muffled and damp, and he couldn't hear John's voice.

He refocused on the PowerPoint. This kind of presentation had become commonplace in the department over the past few years, but it had ramped up even more after the recent stabbing, and the resultant campus-wide initiative, around which an already lucrative bureaucracy had become even more lucrative. That summer had been unseasonably warm, and there had been an uptick in violence all over the country, broadcast live on screens in people's pockets—one killing, then another killing, maybe a response killing; then news and endless chatter, essays and posts and speaking circuits—and Harold's colleagues spent days and weeks and money litigating the ideological justification or the lack thereof for each. The Larmey killing was strangely absent from this discourse, Harold suspected, because the motives were opaque and the victim and perpetrator were the same race, same age, and went to the same school. At Shepherd, the English Department scrambled to align itself with progress. When it came to injustice—such as the injustice that compelled disenfranchised people to commit acts of violence—the important thing was to keep talking and publishing and posting. Authors and academics on all sides set about explaining why these acts were necessary, or the result of certain agentic processes acting upon otherwise good individuals.

The violence that allowed each to condemn his neighbor was always and in every case the most interesting to them.

At Shepherd, violence was bad, but *the right kind* of violence was not violence at all: it was justice, or love. The college and its inhabitants were haunted by a violent past, which manifested as a tortured spirit, traversing generations, passed back and forth among the faculty and students. It wore a different set of symbols every generation or two, but there was no escaping it. The spirit of the past helped create *the spirit of the age*, that frantically deluded ghost that swept through everyone and left them on one side or the other of what people called "history."

John stood at the front of the room, ears drooping like a sick pig.

Harold squinted to read the text next to the word "Defensiveness" at the exact moment John was about to read the text aloud. "Defensiveness," he said, at the same time Harold thought it. "When people, often in power," John said and Harold thought, "are dismissive of new ideas solely for fear that they might shake things up. The defensiveness of people in power creates an oppressive culture."

Harold chewed his cheeks. He flexed and unflexed his biceps in unison.

David was listening attentively. Dolly was listening

attentively. Vance was listening attentively. His cheeks were flushed.

John was on number eleven, "Individualism." Harold read it as he spoke, so that their voices were one. "This idea is found among people who have 'little experience or comfort working as part of a team.' It can lead to isolation, and emphasize competition over cooperation."

Harold looked around the room, scanning hopelessly for Casey. Harold texted him again, asking if he was planning on hitting the gym after the meeting.

Ffff, Harold thought. He gripped the backpack between his feet.

John hiccupped, then yelped. "Fourteen: Right to Comfort," he said. "Those in power may believe that they 'have a right to emotional and psychological comfort,' while denying the same to those not in power. We must remember that 'equating individual acts of unfairness against white people with systematic racism daily targets people of color.'"

Harold wanted to target his pectorals and triceps.

Harold flexed his pecs—right, then left—as he recalled watching his dad make his pecs dance when Harold was a child. Harold's dad often sat on the couch, bouncing his pecs, one at a time, in rhythm with the television. Harold still couldn't make his pecs dance exactly; there was a slight lag between when he willed a contraction in his left pec and when it actually contracted, a body-brain delay that existed more on his left side—his weak side—than his right, which he could make move instantaneously, whenever he so pleased.

Harold envisioned himself doing an incline bench press, then envisioned himself doing dips.

An icy stillness descended on the table. Limbs moved as if in freezing temperatures; faces wincing, forcing smiles—war.

Harold tried to keep his head still on his neck, but it moved up and down instinctively.

When Harold refocused his eyes, John was sitting and Dianthe was at the head of the room.

Dianthe had confided in him weeks prior that she did not like the speaker who was coming, who was white, and who had made a fortune giving talks at universities and companies about antiracism. Dianthe was black, and a Christian, but she was smart, so Harold tried not to hold her Christianity against her. She was talented and wrote brilliantly about many of the things their colleagues jabbered sloppily on about, but her conclusions were overlooked by both her critics and her admirers. Her sci-fi novel, *One Blood*, by far her most popular work, was regarded by almost everyone who read it as a masterpiece for its "investigation" of "the intersection between" various abstractions. After the book came out, Harold heard Sarah tell Dianthe that she was "so moved" by the book, and "simply floored" by the conclusion that "racialized capitalism and patriarchy are so bad in America that the protagonist, in despair, cries out to a nonexistent god." Dolly nodded so hard that Harold feared her head would fall off. She thought it was "just genius" that "even the main character uses the language of the religion of her oppressors to formulate her hope at the end, because it shows just how deep and inescapable the problem is." Dianthe had smiled sympathetically and made the sign of the cross, but made no rebuttal, which Harold found strange.

Dianthe and Harold barely spoke, but Dianthe was exceptionally kind to him too. Harold was unnerved by her kindness. He didn't trust it. He vaguely wished that she would treat him contemptuously, as he felt his other colleagues did. Harold felt some perverse pleasure in the idea of his life getting radically altered at the hands of his adversaries.

He had even been somewhat jealous when, a year prior, Casey was called in for a few meetings about some accusations that had been leveled against him.

Casey had seemed largely unaffected, which Harold admired: Casey seemed set apart. He was not zombified and sterile like the rest of the faculty. For a time, the faculty had fawned over him, and he enjoyed a kind of kingship in the department. His status, and also his easy nature, drew people to him, but his singularity made it difficult to get close to him. Casey wasn't stoic, or even particularly hard to read. It was just that Casey never seemed to *need* anything from other people. One found oneself wanting something from Casey, then wanting more, whereas Casey never needed anything in return. This made people desire him all the more. And it made some people jealous, but they were cunning enough to mask their jealousy with compliments, albeit with certain shaded tones . . .

This is exactly what Nietzsche was talking about, Harold thought, staring at John in his seat. Harold's muscles felt flat and dehydrated. He could actually *feel* them shrinking.

Harold heard John's wetly blinking eye. Perhaps, by some sort of sorcery, Harold thought, his colleagues' eyes dehydrated his muscles: their eyes were wet because they had sucked the water out of Harold's muscles. Perhaps this was also why Harold was becoming weaker at the school: professors had sponge eyes, which they developed from reading only to extract information—which was really more like sucking than reading—and this eye-sucking-reading method evolved to extract muscle water from the strong.

My muscles ... Harold tried to piece together some thoughts that would distract him ... Casey ... he thought, graspingly.

Vance asked if there was any more new business, then reminded everyone that Bri, one of their former colleagues, would be returning for a class visit, to explain her unorthodox interpretation of a little-known text from the Middle Ages to Vance's students. Everything blurred into a sick whirr. Bri, Harold thought, was a *micro fact mincer*, who—

Vance thanked everyone and, adopting a mock-serious air, concluded, "Meeting adjourned."

Harold tried to push David's thermos off the table using only his mind, not thinking he'd be able to do it, and not doing it.

A low murmur emerged as his colleagues all made noises in unison. Harold put his shoe on. Should he wait until everyone else left, so he could stand up with the backpack unnoticed? No. Everyone was caught up in their own little concerns. Just as Harold stood, gripping the backpack and preparing to sling it over his shoulder, he felt a warm hand on his back.

"Hey," a voice cut through the static. Harold turned.

"Hey," he replied, mirroring the tone. It was Vance.

"What are you up to later?" A burst of warmth, perhaps due to the euphoria of the meeting ending, or human touch, permeated Harold's entire being, and Harold reached out and hugged Vance, pulling him in close. Harold's stomach lining sizzled. He felt a chill. He let him go.

"I'm going to the gym," Harold said.

Before Vance could reply, Harold turned and walked away from him.

When Harold traversed the curling halls, backpack strapped around him, he felt like he was skipping, even as he froze in the vestibule, which was probably twenty degrees hotter than the rest of the building, just before going outside, wondering for a moment whether or not his thinking about the sauna had mysteriously "caused" the vestibule to overheat, while also recognizing that this was impossible, as he started singing, slowly, "Casey, Casey, Casey-y-y" under his breath, as he pushed his way out into the cold.

TWO

I

THE PARKING GARAGE ACROSS THE STREET
from the gym was only two stories high. It did not generate the standard sensations of a parking garage; one did not feel that there could be criminals waiting behind smudged columns to senselessly victimize passersby with no one around to see or hear. The parking garage was more like a parking lot with a roof over it, so one felt uncharacteristically exposed in shadowed light, which came in through the wide entrance and wrapped around clean cement columns. There were no tight, dark corners; no disorienting Enter-Exit signs; no jam-packed, too-large vehicles with tinted windows; no dank smell or dark presence.

As Harold sat in his car, eating his protein bar and drinking L-citrulline and beetroot powder, he felt preemptively embarrassed: anyone who came into the parking garage would certainly see him sitting there, and so instead of the parking garage itself feeling creepy, Harold would be the creepy one.

He did not want a pretty girl from the gym to see him sitting there, ferally tearing at a protein bar with his teeth, drinking a disgusting red concoction. He didn't want any of the trainers or strong men to see him either. Harold felt twitchy, like any sudden movement might make him flinch and drop his bar onto his filthy car floor. His thoughts thudded against the silence; they throbbed like little hearts inside his head.

He chugged the rest of his pre-workout, which tasted bitter and warm. Some of it dribbled out of the corners of his mouth onto his shirt. Ggg, he thought, tilting his neck down to glimpse his own collar, on which he could just make out a small red splotch. Harold stuck his tongue out as if he were going to lick it, but as his tongue made contact with the grainy, dry fabric, it quickly recoiled into his mouth.

Harold looked down: gridded images of shirtless muscled men and women's butts in yoga pants appeared as he inched his face toward his phone, using his tongue to remove any remaining globs of protein bar from between his teeth. Harold tapped a video with a shredded woman in the thumbnail: she marched around an empty gym with a barbell on her shoulders; text appeared on the screen, EXCITED TO START DEADLIFTING MORE BECAUSE THEN I'LL GET THAT [PEACH EMOJI]; the video cut to her wearing a tight tank top, flexing her huge arms and shoulders—which Harold passively recognized as the same size as, if not bigger than, his—as the text changed to JUST GETS BIGGER TRAPS with a skull emoji; then the video jump cut to her standing bent over with her arms and head and hair all hanging, slumped. Harold slid his finger up on the screen to scroll to the next video: a black man with dreadlocks squatting 405 pounds while a rap song kept repeating the phrase "How much money you got? A lot."

Harold watched a series of videos in quick succession, letting them play automatically: a blond-haired, blue-eyed bodybuilder posing shirtless, flexing in various positions, with the caption "The old ones say we Spartans are descended from Hercules himself"; a blonde woman standing in a dim gym with a voice-over saying, "You merely adopted the dark; I was born in it" as she removed her hoodie, flexed her biceps, then turned her butt toward the camera; an advertisement for some kind of balm; two youthful brunettes in neon sweats dancing and clapping in front of a body of water with a cityscape behind it; a thin black man bench-pressing on a wide bench, with the overlaid text 330LB BENCH PRESS / SIXTEEN YEARS OLD, and a heavy metal song playing in the background; an Asian toddler in a football jersey, her white mom sitting next to her in another team's jersey, play-menacingly whispering something inaudible with the text WHEN THEY CHOOSE THEIR DAD'S TEAM INSTEAD OF YOURS; an Asian man in a headband using some kind of exercise machine, with the text EASIEST WAY TO LOSE THAT MUFFIN TOP ... then CARDIO 3X PER WEEK then 1-2

GALLONS OF WATER PER DAY then LIFT HEAVY! overlaid on the video one after the other; a black woman shaking a bottle of orange liquid in a shaker cup, with the text YOU GO TO THE GYM TOO MUCH overlaid on the video, and audio of a man saying "La la la la—shhh—living my life" playing over it.

Harold shook his cup, then took a sip, remembering, as the sandy remains of beetroot powder touched his gums, that he'd already finished. He turned his torso, sputtering and grimacing and licking his gums, and fished an old plastic water bottle from the floor behind him. He swished stale water in his mouth and then swallowed.

As he turned again to toss the water bottle onto the floor behind him, Harold saw the backpack, sitting on the back seat, leaned against the door. The backpack looked sad, sitting there, slumped like that.

Harold decided to sit in his car for another minute or two. Food wasn't converted into energy until thirty or forty minutes after eating, he knew, so the protein bar he'd eaten wouldn't even physically affect his workout—waiting an extra minute wouldn't give anything time to digest, and in fact may even hinder his body's performance, because it would have to expend extra energy on digesting the protein bar—but his brain had its own strained logic: Harold would "feel fuller," having eaten, and so would have a better workout. Harold tried to forget about the congealed vegetable oil the bar contained, the tortured process by which oil was squeezed out of non-oily vegetables and seeds, using mechanized, industrial processes and heat to create a product that could be put into literally anything and cause all sorts of health problems when consumed in large quantities. He tried to forget about the fact that, besides the twenty grams of protein, the bar was not helping him in any way. In fact, it was probably hurting him: the vegetable oil damaged cellular communication, and changed the way genes were expressed; as a result, his children—if he ever had children—could be deformed, or autistic.

A black sedan crept slowly into the garage. Harold could make out the dim outlines of heads and shoulders inside, looking through his side- and rear-view mirrors. He quickly checked his email, closed his email, then opened and closed his email again, and when he looked up and away—still feeling beet powder sediment on his gums, and baring his teeth in the rearview to check—he noticed that the black sedan still hadn't parked, but was inching by, slowed now to a near stop behind him.

There were plenty of places to park. What was going on? Casey had a black sedan. Or was it blue? Harold sank down into his seat, eyeing the car through the side view, eager to catch Casey in the act, but just as he sank down, it sped up and disappeared around the corner.

Harold tapped Instagram, went to his "Explore" page, then tapped an infographic.

THE THREE A'S, it said at the top, with a numbered list beneath—1. ASSESS 2. ACCEPT 3. ACT—overlaid on a cartoon bodybuilder. He swiped down to the next video: a girl doing glute exercises in yoga pants, her butt taking up the entire frame. Harold watched the glute video twice, then scrolled down—a giant, shirtless European man doing shoulder presses and repeatedly yelling "Yessir."

Harold scrolled—an ad; an image of a coiling fire hose—then looked at the time: five minutes had passed since he'd parked. How was this possible? Time had slunk by impossibly slowly—now it was disappearing; Harold was burning energy just sitting there—fff, ggghh—he twisted his torso and grabbed his gym bag, smelling the stale air as he pulled it forward, sour sweat and faint remnants of tea tree oil, which he'd lazily sprinkled into the bag to mask the odor, rising up into his nostrils. He pictured the female employee who sometimes worked at the front desk—would she smell it when he passed?

Harold emptied out the contents of his gym bag in a fevered rush: he could transfer his belongings to the backpack and use that as his gym bag instead. Harold grabbed the backpack, lifted it to his nose, and inhaled. Finally—a purpose. None of Harold's colleagues except Casey had a gym membership, so none of his colleagues except Casey could potentially catch him with the backpack. Harold was in the clear.

He took out the "marginalized identities" poster, two notebooks, two library books—*The Screwtape Letters* by C. S. Lewis and the National Audubon Society's *Field Guide to Reptiles and Amphibians*—a laptop and a charger, a stack of envelopes that appeared unused, despite having the same address scrawled on each of them—pens and a few crumpled pieces of paper, five protein bar wrappers, and he stuffed them all beneath his passenger seat. Maybe he could turn the laptop in, he thought, and say he'd found it somewhere—the bathroom? A twinge of guilt passed over him—what if the student hadn't backed up his files?—but he quickly pushed it down as he removed another notebook from the backpack.

Then Harold—as if having some presentiment—lowered his hand in, with trepidation.

Harold's hand descended until it encountered something smooth and cool, like stone. He traced his finger along the flat surface. The feeling of the object moved up his forearm—but stayed below his elbow, and nothing registered—until he met an edge and felt that he might cut himself. Harold gently pressed his pointer finger against the edge. He pressed down harder. He lifted his hand out of the bag and looked at his finger: he could see the fine lines of his fingerprint, obscured by the indentation that the object had made. He reached back in and traced the edge again, searching for a point. Nothing. Then his hand found something slightly more rectangular, and firm—he gripped it and pulled up.

The object moved smoothly; Harold felt as if he were pulling a sword out of a stone. Here was the shiny object after all. Harold had been right! A familiar satisfaction rose in him as the silvery blade emerged from the backpack, and Harold's heart beat quickly in the base of his throat.

Harold held the knife out in front of him. He turned it in the shadowed light. It wasn't silver, exactly, but gray. He lifted it up so he could see it better, then shot his hand down in case anyone was looking through the car window. Harold glanced around, then lifted it again. He brought the object closer to his face. It was a knife—but it wasn't like any knife he'd ever seen. It was thin, lighter than a butter knife—it had none of the weight of something that could kill. But could it kill? Harold felt the dull edge and pressed. He pressed harder. He remembered learning that in order to bite into a finger, one had only to apply the same amount of force as biting into a carrot. Why did this student have such a dull knife?

Harold looked around his car for a place to safely stash it, scanning bottles, notebooks, wrappers; then he saw the envelopes peeking out from beneath the seat—a letter opener—no—paper knife. This was a paper knife, a damask paper knife; Harold had read about these—they were old; the blade was made of stone. The student must have used it to open the letters. Harold grinned.

Harold placed the knife in the cupholder and began transferring the contents of his gym bag into the backpack. The crosses swung back and forth as he stuffed his belongings down into the bag. This cuck, Harold scoffed, seeing the crosses. I took his backpack, and what? He will already have forgiven me!

Harold mentally projected a series of faces he had seen in the halls that day. He imagined them all murmuring "I forgive you," as he towered over them and made them bow. I am teaching, he thought as he gripped the zipper between his fingers and zipped it closed, even now.

Harold heard a car door close behind him and flinched. In the rearview, two giggling girls got out of a dark green Honda Civic, carrying gym bags. Harold held the paper knife loosely, and felt a kind of affection for it; the smooth stone handle reminded him of rocks in the woods behind the house where he grew up; as a kid, he would throw them at trees and think warmly about the faces of the girls he had crushes on—he'd play a game where if he hit three trees in a row, the girls would like him back, and he would stay out there throwing rocks and fantasizing about kissing their cheeks and hands, aiming for particular beech trees in the distance, until it got too dark to see. The paper knife felt cool in his hand—images of childhood welling up in him—the face of a friend who had gotten a girlfriend, then slowly stopped hanging out with him—one of his teachers who encouraged him to write poems—the pavilion next to the pond where he'd sit alone when he told his parents he was going bowling. Without thinking, he stabbed the paper knife into the bottom of the passenger seat, and tore a little at the fabric. Then he pulled it out and put it back into the backpack.

II

THE GLISTENING SECOND-STORY FLOOR-TO-
ceiling windows of Hill's Health World seemed to radiate a kind of life, shining outward from surrounding
brick, drowning everything with its illuminated sign:
"HILL's." The sign was from the original location, when
the gym had been called Pheath Hill's Weight Dun-
geon—a name that the owners must have realized would
be prudent to change once the gym became a place for
everyone—and so now only the "Hill's" remained.

Harold walked slowly, so as to remain at a distance
from the giggling girls, who were likely already inside
but who, Harold considered, may have stopped briefly
to tie their shoes or check their phones or talk—
women, Harold noticed, often stopped walking when
they had something important to say, or when they got
too wrapped up in conversation generally, standing

in the middle of the street or on a crowded sidewalk, forcing others to go around them—and so he wanted to take this possibility into account.

Harold's thoughts felt like air coated in sludge. Everything felt brighter with his face in the cold sun. The Three A's, he thought, absently. His colleagues did not follow the Three A's . . . More like the Three . . . He was unable to think.

Phantom fragments of John and his PowerPoint, as well as other random, slivered images from the meeting—Kirk's coming in late, the phrase "reduced graduate admissions"—still lingered as his thoughts swelled and contracted like a stomach—Harold could not think—the Three . . .

The weights are not to blame, he thought, quoting another caption he'd seen on Instagram, half-heartedly trying to redeem his aborted "Three A's" joke, and looking up at Hill's, grasping at other slogans like he was scrolling through his mind. The weights are not . . . the Three . . .

Harold's thoughts felt simultaneously thick and thin; airy, but coated in sludge. Harold's thoughts lived in the top of his head. The sludge carried them down toward his face, but they were disconnected from the rest of him. He couldn't feel them anywhere—he couldn't feel his thoughts.

Weights, he thought, but the thought stayed at the top of his head. It did not come down into his face. His scalp tingled. Harold squinted in the cold sun, crossing the street.

His colleagues, with the exception of Casey, were

constantly shaking their fists at the weights, he thought, feeling the sludge come down now; if his colleagues ever stepped into Hill's, he thought, it would only be a matter of time until they were rearranging all the dumbbells nonsensically, so that the eighty-pound dumbbells were next to the fifteen-pound dumbbells, and the twenty-five-pound dumbbells were next to the hundred-pound dumbbells, and so on . . .

Scatterers and blunderers, he thought, disgruntled. They take anything whole and make it many; anything unified and break it into tiny chunks . . .

Harold tried to formulate his thoughts in the rhythm of a rap song—"Anything whole and make it many tiny chunks"; "Any-thing-chunks"—but he couldn't make it rhyme.

Perhaps, he reconsidered, feeling the weight of the backpack shift, his colleagues would merely switch the order of the weights, so that instead of starting with the largest weights and going down, they'd start with the smallest and go up. Weak people think backward, he thought. People were born with backward brains, and they didn't get turned around until after they started to lift.

A black cardboard cutout of a strong male physique loomed over the lobby as Harold entered the revolving door. The faceless silhouette held a barbell, which bent cartoonishly due to the amount of weight on either end.

Sometimes, when Harold entered the gym, he would contemplate the shape of the cutout's muscles— the fullness of the capped, boulder-esque deltoids; the massive lats, like slabs, creating an inverted triangle-shaped back; the dips between the shoulder and biceps; the girthy, bulbous, heart-shaped calves; quadriceps like chicken breasts ballooning out from beneath the small, supple waist—but today, he noticed the shape of the head. The head wasn't particularly large or small. In fact, the head was absolutely unremarkable. One might imagine, Harold considered while scaling the flight of stairs, that the artist would have given the man a giant, veiny, near-bursting head. In real life, when one lifted bar-bending weight, one's head invariably looked like it was going to explode—although, Harold thought, of course, this was due to the reddish-purpling of the face, or the veininess, which would be impossible to render in an all-black cutout. Alternatively, Harold considered, it wouldn't have been surprising if the artist had given him a comically small head, to emphasize the largeness of the muscles—but no, he had a right-sized head. Because of this fact, Harold reflected, the silhouette was almost somber. A perfectly proportioned physique with a right-sized head—quite the normal, and indeed unremarkable, head—gave the physique an eerie seriousness, as opposed to other gym logos, made by lesser gym logo artists, who opted for something cartoonish and ridiculous.

In his memoir, Mel used the term "right-sized" fairly regularly; the seventh chapter in the book was called "Becoming Right-Sized." The title was somewhat of a joke, since until this point Mel had been single-mindedly focused on becoming the biggest bodybuilder to have ever lived, but now, having won countless competitions, and suffering from panic attacks, Mel needed something new. This part of Mel's life and career had been unfortunate—perhaps the steroids had made him crazy—but now, considering the cardboard cutout, Harold understood: lifting weights resulted in giant muscles, but giant muscles resulted in a right-sized head.

There was a pernicious misconception among non-lifters that people with beautiful physiques were egotistical and vain, when in reality the opposite was true: men with stacked and succulent muscles and a low body fat percentage were the most humble people in the world. When you wanted to discern someone's spiritual condition, Harold thought, considering the cutout, all you had to do was consider their heads. David's head ballooned up and then deflated; Dolly's wide cranium jutted down into a tiny jaw, like an alien's; John's scrunched and squinty countenance twitched like it got zapped into every expression; Vance's head was perfectly square. When a person lives proudly within his spiritual malady, he flaunts this in his physical features, primarily in the shape of his head, thereby imposing his sickness onto others. But this was not the case with lifters, whose heads, as the silhouette so eloquently demonstrated, were the perfect size.

Humility, the shape of the head seemed to suggest, was the first thing one learned in the gym, where one either humbles himself or gets humbled. A new lifter is never as strong as he imagines; he is weak, and ignorant; movements that had seemed simple turn out to be surprisingly complex. In the gym, either one learns how to lift properly—using light weights initially and asking for help—or gets injured. In both cases, humility is the mechanism by which the lifter grows. This is why lifters level epithets like "ego lifter" at each other: humility, not pride, is the arch virtue of the lifter.

As Harold approached the top of the staircase, he took his keys out of his pocket and got his key tag ready, facing away from him.

III

OFTEN, ONE RECEIVES GLIMPSES OF WHAT'S to come, as if the future travels back into the past, bringing with it some kind of message, a premonition or presentiment, which appears half-concealed, as through a reflection in a dark screen.

Harold saw Casey in the distance, twisted up. His mangled body lay on the ground in a heap of gnarled flesh, his legs pretzeled and raised, arms straight back past his head. Harold reached for his phone to call for help—did Casey have a seizure? had someone killed him?—and focused his eyes: a rowing machine. The matte black floor met the shiny black and tan machines, giving them a slight gleam, like apparitions calling out. Though Harold had never used the rowing machines, he now felt drawn to them. Occasionally, things appear as more than objects, imbued with some spirit that attracts us to them, and we do not choose, so much as we are pulled toward them, into a future we could not have planned or reasoned our way into. We make choices, but these choices are not the result of reasoned deliberation; rather, we feel compelled by something, or toward something, for reasons that are ultimately obscure, and we rationalize our actions afterward.

No one was at the desk when Harold scanned in. In the distance, a few employees congregated around a high desk with a computer, talking to a woman, who was presumably inquiring about membership, all laughing and showing their teeth.

Harold had been coming to Hill's for three years, and though he hadn't developed any relationships he would describe as "friendships," he was familiar enough with the employees that they nodded or touched knuckles when they passed. Before Harold started lifting, he went about his days like a ghost. When he was not at Shepherd, no one would speak to him, except to say "Cash or card?" or "Will that be all for you today?"

It wasn't until coming to Hill's that Harold started to feel part of something. The person at the front desk would say "Have a good workout" or "Good to see you again," and when he'd leave they'd ask him how his workout went, or tell him to have a good day, and it confirmed his existence. It was a small thing, but life was made of small things.

Cal was his favorite Hill employee. He was the only one who knew Harold by name. Cal's physique was decent, lean, natural. His glutes were his best feature—Cal looked like he had two Christmas hams stuffed in the back of his shorts. Whenever Harold walked past Cal, it took an enormous effort not to turn and gawk at his glutes, which were always prominently displayed in tight-fitting shorts. Women online often complained about men staring at them in the gym, and Harold often felt piggish for looking—usually quickly and involuntarily, something primal in him activated by the skin and the tight spandex that outlined the body in extraordinary detail—before looking away, but he was pleased to notice that it wasn't just the female glutes his eyes were naturally drawn to: Harold wasn't an animal; he was a person, with an aesthetic appreciation of glutes themselves.

Cal often trained old ladies, and Harold frequently overheard Cal discussing some trifle with one or another of them.

Now Cal stood laughing near the high desk. Cal was short, perhaps only five foot eight, but the trainer standing next to him was even shorter: he came up only to Cal's shoulder. This was Harold's least favorite Hill employee. He looked like ground meat squeezed within a giant fist, then haphazardly molded into a vaguely human shape. He had one giant dreadlock that hung down like a rope. He waddled, barely able to turn his chunky body, and he always wore cologne that lingered when he was no longer there, such that even if Harold couldn't see him, he could walk into a wall of scent and know that this unseemly, grotesque trainer was nearby.

Once, Harold saw him doing an exercise with one of his young trainees where he put an exercise band around her waist like a lasso and she walked forward as he pulled back on the band, shouting "Giddyup! Go! Go!" as she pushed forward through his resistance.

In front of the computer stood a third employee, who wore a giant silver cross around his neck. Tall, lean, broad shoulders, thin waist. Harold grasped the backpack straps below his shoulders.

As Harold looked on the scene at the high desk, he caught himself smiling, briefly trying to discern the attractiveness of the woman standing with them, as well as whether she was signing up for a monthly pass or a day pass; hoping, in some distant and only semi-articulated way, that Cal would nod at him or acknowledge his presence in some way, maybe with a wave, as he'd done so many times before; Harold wanted his first impression on the potential new member to be that of someone who was casually waved at, someone whom people, even when they were working, interrupted themselves to greet.

Harold walked toward the locker room.

IN THE PUBLIC imagination, men's locker rooms were places in which homoerotic towel snappers played practical jokes on each other, where hazing rituals established a pecking order among men amid the musty smell of hairy skin and cheap soap.

For young boys, locker rooms were essentially new wombs. They were left alone together for perhaps the first time in their lives, unobserved by adults or girls, and they scrambled like embryonic DNA to find their place in this new order. Under these conditions, young boys became themselves: some were violent, some were quiet, some pulled their pants all the way down around their ankles when they peed. Eyes became furtive measurers, darting cautiously, lids slid half-closed so as to hide from view the pupils' true direction.

But an adult male locker room was not this way at all. Most men moved with purpose, as if entirely unaware of their surroundings or each other. In a youth locker room, everyone was painfully visible; in an adult locker room, everyone was familiarly invisible. Some older men even seemed to savor their time there, retrieving their deodorant or phone in slow motion, as if each movement—taking their bag out of the locker, then their watch out of the bag; putting the watch on their wrist, snapping the band shut—was among the most pleasurable activities in the world.

At this stage, men were less confused about who they were in relation to each other, and so if they didn't look at each other, they didn't even really see each other: eyes met, heads nodded, friendly regulars straightforwardly commented on each other's bodies ("Looking huge!"; "Hey, big man!"), but it was always only a gesture toward what was essentially an outline—shape and size—and never something concrete and specific, like the emergence of a new vein visible in their shoulder, or a greater separation between the two main muscles in the quadricep . . .

As Harold entered the locker room, he perceived himself as "looking like a student," due to his
new backpack, and he moved quickly; black lockers,
stacked two high, towered over him; bright light shot
down from above but also seemed to shine up from
the floor, and Harold had the sensation of being suspended in space. He opened a locker, and for a moment felt as if he might fall into it; the surrounding
light was sucked deep into the rectangular compartment, such that when he threw his keys into it, they
seemed as if they might get sucked all the way down
into some unending, uninhabited abyss.

Harold's phone vibrated as he pulled off his pants:
a text from David, calling John "out of his mind." Harold hated getting texts from David. He hated getting
texts from any of his colleagues except Casey. Why
hadn't Casey texted him back? How had David even
gotten his number? Harold couldn't help feeling like
David was secretly plotting against him, and that every interaction they had had was just a cunning step
in his grand plan. Ever since their first encounter, David had been nice to Harold, and it was precisely this
niceness that was so brutal. Harold could see through
it like water. Even in this attempt to connect over text,
David had to reach his wretched hand up and try to
pull another colleague down.

Those stuck down in their pits, Harold thought,
with raised hands grasping up, can only ever pull others down. Harold envisioned David's hand reaching
out of the backpack as he reached into it—mindful
of the paper knife—and carefully removed his gym

clothes. People sometimes appear as if they're reaching out for help, Harold thought, but in reality they don't want help, and are not even aware that they need help, and they just want to hurt someone. Pit people like David want company in their pit—and nothing more.

Harold's phone buzzed again. He clenched his teeth. Wh . . . he thought. He folded his pants and put them in the locker.

Despite David's repellent nature, a part of Harold still wanted to respond, as if wondering, upon seeing a giant flame, what would happen if he passed his hand through it.

Choices build on top of each other until they don't feel like choices but like *the way things are*, Harold reminded himself as he slipped into his shorts, then shimmied into his T-shirt. Decisions compound until they feel like external forces—and by that point, in some sense, they are.

Thus, Harold would not respond. He tied his shoes and closed his locker. Then he opened the locker and slid his phone under his clothes. The screen lit up as he moved it, displaying the same texts from David again.

No, Harold thought. Life was not one big thing but an interconnected assemblage of innumerable little things. Harold's life consisted of millions of concrete choices, and he refused to let them stack up and topple over onto him. He refused to let them topple over onto anyone else either. Weakness always off-loaded itself onto innocent victims; Harold would handle each and every small decision; he would not respond; he would not give his energy away. He would instead choose nobly.

Harold grabbed his phone from the locker—he would need it to double-check his exercises for today—and walked purposefully out into the gym.

IV
##

IN THE LOBBY, HAROLD WALKED PAST RACKS of snacks and powders—protein, amino acids, some type of crackers, all branded with psychotic fonts with pointy edges and dripping letters—and out into the gym. He texted David, "Hah."

The front of the gym was wide open, an uncluttered expanse of black flooring for calisthenics: at the center of the clearing was an enclosed rectangle of black bars perpendicular to the floor, held up by black steel beams, with rings attached to ropes hanging off certain parts. To the left was a matted section that had the word STRETCH stenciled on the wall above a full-length mirror, where a few girls did glute and core exercises, wriggling on the floor like kids being tickled.

Harold was pleased to see no men in that section. He often saw large men doing crunches and sit-ups like maniacs, drenched in sweat, grunting, hoping to get a chiseled midsection, when this was for the most part hopeless: the visibility of abs was almost exclusively dependent on one's body fat percentage. Of course, one needed some musculature in order to have visible abs, but stabilizing during heavy lifts provided more than enough stimulation to the abdominal muscles. Even though the sign above the matted section said STRETCH, it could have more appropriately said VANITY, because that was where people went to exercise their glutes and abs.

Harold walked past rows of cardio equipment: treadmills, elliptical machines, StairMasters, "Jacob's Ladder" (which he'd never seen anyone use, but which, he inferred from its shape and appearance, functioned like a treadmill for climbing on all fours). Six large flat-screens hung on the wall facing the treadmills: a football game, two news stations, a daytime drama, commercials, all with subtitles. The cardio machines were basically unoccupied, with the exception of some women jogging and an obese man wobbling on an elliptical machine.

The obese man had been coming for months, and it made Harold enormously happy. There was nothing so pleasing as seeing a fat person at the gym. Often, in this gluttonous and poisoned country, where the food and the water and the people's minds were poisoned, people became fat in childhood and stayed fat for their whole lives, becoming fatter and fatter, then plateauing at a certain level before dying. With each new pound gained, Harold imagined, it became harder to get oneself to go to the gym, and Harold commended and respected those who did.

The obese man's flesh flung up around his bones beneath his sweat-soaked shirt, his face a determined grimace, and Harold revered him, perceiving him as being in an action movie.

Bright white light showered the black and silver machines, which appeared like the limbs of an invisible body. The machines seemed sterile, which was one of the downsides of new commercial gyms: the equipment appeared cosmetic, like Botox—something meant to simulate life, but not life.

The weights themselves, however, were not simulations, no matter how new they looked: one forty-five-pound plate weighed the same as every other forty-five-pound plate, and everyone who lifted one forty-five-pound plate lifted the same amount of weight. In this way, due to their rigid objectivity, weights were also the great equalizer, even as they resulted in a hierarchy.

To Harold's relief, one of the two deadlift platforms in the corner was unoccupied. On the other platform was a strong twentysomething-year-old. Harold didn't look at the young man's bar long enough to inspect it, but it had at least four plates on either side of it. He claimed his spot on the platform next to the window and warmed up: swinging each leg side to side, then front to back; standing straight and consciously contracting his glutes for fifteen seconds; swinging and circling his arms; shrugging with his arms at his sides; shrugging with his arms raised above him; circling his neck. Harold approached the bar, performed fifteen deadlift repetitions with it, then started adding weight, performing three to six reps each time, until he had 405 pounds on the bar—the same as what his askance look at the young man beside him indicated he was lifting.

Harold's plan was to work up to a weight where he could do four sets of two reps, something sufficiently challenging but where he wouldn't fail. He wanted to build strength, and in order to do that he had to be smart about the amount of effort he exerted.

In the past, Harold had trained as hard as he could every session, because that is what he read online to do, but as the weeks went on, he made no progress, and some days he was even weaker than before.

This was because he had misunderstood something fundamental. He didn't understand the difference between training for strength and training for size. This subtle difference was elucidated when he spent more time watching YouTube. When training for hypertrophy—muscle growth—as opposed to brute strength, it was important to get as close to failure as possible, with lighter weight, in a higher rep range, to stimulate growth; but for strength, one had to strategically, and counterintuitively, work at submaximal effort—with higher weight, for lower reps—so as not to fry the central nervous system.

There were many different training styles, and Harold was still a relatively new lifter—he'd been lifting for four years—so he had incorporated aspects of different styles into his training: he generally trained heavy at the beginning of the workout, and lighter but with higher intensity for the remainder.

Like Casey, who had used the phrase when he taught Harold how to bench, Harold did not want what were essentially "show muscles," which looked aesthetically pleasing but which were secretly weak. However, like Casey, Harold did not want to become bloated and gross like many powerlifters. Bodybuilders and powerlifters were more alike than different—especially compared to non-lifters—but there was often intense conflict among them. Bodybuilders wanted to be big, whereas powerlifters wanted to be strong, and this created an irreconcilable rift between them. But Harold had a simple solution: he would become both big and strong. If it weren't for Casey, he wouldn't have known what he wanted, but after Casey explained it to him and Harold spent more time on YouTube, it seemed the most natural thing in the world, like the desire had always been in him.

Once, in the sauna, Casey and Harold had debated whether it was better to be a bodybuilder or a powerlifter. Harold had often imagined himself on various panels, debating various *scholarly issues*, but he never thought he'd find himself in earnest debating these kinds of questions too. The sauna had been a shocking revelation for Harold: the way men talked about the news, or politics, or their jobs, was more profound and philosophical than the way his colleagues at Shepherd talked. At first, Harold contended that it was better to be a powerlifter, because powerlifters were strong, and it was more useful to be strong, but Casey said that it was better to be a bodybuilder, because bodybuilders were still stronger than 99.9 percent of people, but they also looked good, which was important.

Many powerlifters, Casey said, seemed to reject physical beauty, opting for what they viewed as a more spiritual kind of beauty, or a more *manly* kind of beauty—the beauty of lifting heavy weights. But this was actually more primitive, Casey contended, and, therefore more *feminine*. A big strong man with a bulbous bloated belly was like a woman, he had said. Consciousness did not progress so that one could reject it and return to what was essentially mammalian: we should delight in higher-order values like beauty, Casey said, and not fall into the trap of mere usefulness.

Harold added more weight to the bar, then performed three deadlift repetitions with ease. He added more, then, after waiting two minutes, did one more repetition. This time it was challenging. Harold stepped back from the bar. He'd done more weight in the past, for more reps, but he was tired, and not properly fueled . . .

Harold added ten pounds total; ten pounds was nothing, he assured himself—although ten pounds was sometimes enough to make all the difference. Harold shook his legs. He did one rep. The bar moved like a knife through butter.

The acute and frenzied suffering Harold had felt less than an hour ago immediately transformed into something more manageable. Even just warming up made him feel less crazed, less oppressed by the Lawes halls.

A familiar urge worked its way into Harold, which, upon acknowledging it, Harold sensed he would not be able to shake. He greeted it with trepidation, then delight—Harold wanted to hit a personal record, a "PR."

The kid on the platform next to him prepared for a deadlift. Harold watched him in the mirror. Harold took the twenty-five- and ten-pound plates off each side of the bar and added another forty-five-pound plate. He could do one here, to build confidence, he considered, then add more? Often, when he added too much weight at once, especially during a PR attempt, he failed. It was already psychologically challenging enough to attempt a PR, especially a PR on a whim, under suboptimal conditions. He could not fail. It would ruin the rest of the workout.

So Harold would build up to it. First, he'd lift an amount he'd previously lifted, to build confidence.

But what if he failed even this one? Failing previously lifted amounts could be debilitating too, even more debilitating than failing a new PR. As Harold stood staring at it, the dreaded prior PR—495 pounds—he changed his mind again: it wouldn't be worth it just to match his previous PR. He had to increase the weight. A new PR, he hoped, would erase the meeting and all of Shepherd from his memory. Harold would decimate any remnants of what still lurked inside him. Harold envisioned himself telling Casey about his PR. He felt giddy. He imagined himself as Casey—Casey could lift this weight easily.

Harold added five pounds to each side—505 pounds. He shook his arms and legs and stared down at the bar. Fffgghhh, he thought, trying to hype himself up. He glanced over at the kid next to him—then looked away.

Fff, he thought. Okay. Five . . . His thoughts had a purgatorial quality; tinny pop music played softly from the speakers, and he regretted not bringing his headphones. He'd need to psych himself up some other way. Fffggg, he thought, flicking his wrists and ankles, slapping his thighs. He picked up his weight belt. Up, he thought, staring down at the weight, wrapping the belt around his midsection, to protect his spine and help him generate more power—you got this.

A random memory of Vance picking up a pencil off the ground and inspecting it and then putting it in his breast pocket entered Harold's mind. He stared at the bar, thinking "pencil," and unintentionally imagined himself as Vance. He glanced again at the kid next to him. The bar is a pencil, he thought, trying to keep everything in him driving toward one thing. But the thought was too effortful; it felt awkward and forced. He was suddenly second-guessing everything. He should have just left Lawes before the meeting, he considered, and gone home to eat; then he'd certainly be able to lift 505 pounds. Why hadn't he just skipped the meeting? He could feel the oil from the protein bar oozing thickly through him. His genes were damaged; his future kids would be ugly. Why couldn't Harold be one of those guys who thrived when he worked out fasted? Harold scrolled through a list of famous lifters in his head who did not eat until the evening and could lift enormous weight. As Harold thought of each lifter, he tried to imagine himself as each of them, as if by simply thinking of them he could suck some of their strength into himself, harness some of their being as his own. Harold adjusted the belt one notch looser, then readjusted it to where it was. Harold breathed his belly out into the belt and thought to loosen it again. The kid next to him had taken some weight off the bar and was now performing deadlift after deadlift with ease. He had blond hair, smooth skin—what if he watched Harold, who was disheveled and old in comparison, fail? Harold had promised himself he wouldn't try to hit a PR for at least another month. He hadn't eaten enough and wouldn't be able to generate enough power. He wasn't caffeinated. He could almost certainly hit this under optimal conditions, but now—

Ffff, he thought, sucking his cheeks, then puffing them out. Was he still another lifter, or had he switched back to Vance, or maybe—he dared not even consider it—himself?

He absently scanned the gym, and saw Mike, a professional bodybuilder whom Harold knew from the sauna, walking toward the area with the machines, then disappearing around a corner.

Harold shook his head. What if he couldn't get it up and someone saw? What if Mike came back this way?

Harold's mind moved quickly, flitting between thoughts noncommittally: images of Vance, famous lifters, Mike. Every thought that wasn't about the lift would bump up against the lift-thought and fall away: Mike; decisecond of projected embarrassment; successful lift; girl in periphery; mirror; Vance with pencil; John. His thoughts weren't even thoughts so much as augmented instincts, cramming concepts and memories onto the stimulus around him in an associative manner. His blood was pumping. What was the worst that could happen? Harold didn't want to think about the worst that could happen. Thinking about the worst that could happen was a loser mentality. Harold was strong. He was not like his colleagues, always catastrophizing over this or that worst-case scenario, projecting it out into the future, *creating* what they feared by focusing on it.

If Harold saw someone fail a 505-pound deadlift, he thought, he wouldn't judge them. Or, he would judge them, but he would judge them positively: 505 pounds was an impressive weight. And even if it wasn't 505 pounds, he considered, but 365 pounds, or even 165 pounds, he would still commend them for failing, because trying to do something beyond one's current capacity—struggling upward, he thought—was commendable. Failure was a part of the process. Failure was, in this sense, good. Harold, no matter what happened, was doing the right thing.

Fffff, he thought. He was already rationalizing failure. He looked out the window and down toward the parking garage. A numb calm washed over him, like he was not in the gym but rather nowhere, dumbly hovering in space, staring down. He turned and addressed the weight. Okay, he thought. You got this.

Easy.

Harold walked up to the weight and slid his feet under the bar. He exhaled and shook his hands. He tried to imagine lifting the weight, but there was a blockage somewhere in him, such that when he tried to imagine the weight going up, he couldn't see it clearly; he couldn't even "see" the weight as he was staring at it—he could only think the command, *imagine lifting the weight*, and the weight itself was invisible, having become an abstract duty, or fear. He breathed in and out twice quickly. He hip-hinged, bent his knees, and gripped the bar with his right palm facing him and his left palm facing out—a "mixed grip"—thinking, Fff, ggghh; he exhaled and inhaled again, pushing his belly out into the belt.

Harold thought about wedging his hips between the bar and the floor, generating force through his feet, pulling with his arms while pushing his glutes and hamstrings forward. He imagined pulling the floor up with the bar and ascending through the ceiling—but the bar didn't budge. He pushed through his legs with the full force of his body. Ffffff. He craned his neck and looked at himself in the mirror—the bar remained still on the ground, and then moved.

He pulled the bar up—it was rising, albeit slowly—and for a moment he was nothing—all muscle and movement—until he came back into himself, and this self-awareness was enough to stop the movement—he dropped the bar when it reached his knees. He exhaled, *fffuuu*, and shook his head. The second of stillness between when he started to pull and when the bar left the ground had caught him off guard, wrecking his focus; in the brief moment before the bar moved, doubt crept in and ruined him.

Fffff, he thought.

He shook his head.

Fffff. Shhfff.

He resolved to try again, then just as quickly decided against it. He paced around, shaking his arms and his head; he projected himself into the future, but the weight didn't leave the floor; he could have done it, he thought, if he hadn't second-guessed himself mid-lift. He'd been so close.

Harold inhaled and exhaled a few times rapidly, like a panting dog. He simply didn't have it in him. He was too tired, or hungry. His central nervous system was too fried. He hadn't slept well enough. The spike in cortisol during the meeting had affected him negatively. Casey wasn't there to encourage him. There were too many distractions.

Past failures floated in and out of Harold's head as he removed the weight from both ends of the bar, feeling dejected, but also good, from the endorphins. Circling, conflicting thoughts consumed him as he hung the plates on pegs attached to the squat rack, then began his trek toward the benches. The deadlift was superfluous anyway; it wasn't actually a part of his program; he was just doing it to build a little strength, and certainly the heavy deads he'd done in preparation for the PR counted for something—even the failed PR attempt itself wasn't a total failure; he had, at least, gotten it off the ground, and pushed his body to do something difficult in the process.

As he passed the water fountains, he noticed a woman, hunched, drinking from the shorter of the two. The energized, unthinking part of Harold bar-reled toward the taller fountain to drink next to the woman, but his feet came to a jolting stop: gym eti-quette in this instance had always been unclear to him. Often, when he drank next to someone, he noticed that they would finish right away, sometimes even standing up as he bent over, such that when he pushed the lever on the water fountain it seemed not only to shoot out water but also to eject the person drinking next to him. People didn't, generally speaking, stand hunched over water fountains for more than a few sec-onds at a time anyway, Harold reasoned, and in any case, he didn't want to crowd this woman out. She seemed unquenchably thirsty, gulping feverishly from the fountain with a rounded, sweaty back.

Perhaps she had just gotten out of a class, Har-old considered: sweaty women were almost always coming from a class, where an instructor led them through a series of jumps, sprints, and light dumb-bell workouts. Harold often saw them in the room next to the free weights, flailing to thumping music, instructor yelling "Woo!" or "Ten more seconds!" as their red faces sputtered and their sticky, meaty bod-ies flopped around.

Harold did not want to awkwardly brush up against her sweaty waist or, worse, accidentally get tickled by her hair, wet strands of which hung loosely against the adjacent fountain. Harold jerked as if he were going to drink next to her, then stopped. The woman paused mid-sip to turn her head, eying Harold as he stood completely still.

The woman took another couple of sips, then shot up like a snapped rubber band. She turned her torso and neck quickly, like a released spring, and gestured toward the water fountain.

Ffff, Harold thought. She had noticed him. "I wasn't hurrying," Harold sputtered, instantaneously pained by this strange outburst. "I mean, feel free to keep drinking," he said, making it worse. He tried to smile warmly, but his lips quivered, so he averted eye contact. He stepped forward, hunched, and took six long sips from the fountain, staring down into the wet, pale gray. Why did he have to be so weird?

The water moving through him felt great. He felt as if he'd jumped into a river, but the river was inside him. He walked to the bench area, which was wide open, only a few people using dumbbells on the far side of the room. The incandescent benches appeared like strips of road. Hot light shone through windows, covering everything—Harold felt like he was standing in the middle of his own heart. The silver barbells and black benches, all evenly spaced in a row, were not like the plastic benches in the Lawes basement, scattered incoherently, like someone had spilled them out of a bag; rather, the workout benches inhered in them a kind of order, a purpose that asserted itself when you looked at them.

Harold picked the bench closest to the window and lay back to warm up, but when he looked up at the bar the sun blinded him. The warm rays felt like an itchy blanket on his skin. He scooted out from under the bar and moved over to the next bench, out of the sun.

He warmed up until he had two forty-five-pound plates on either side of the bar: 225 pounds.

Certain milestones are universally recognized in lifting, specific weights for specific lifts that qualify one as a real lifter. These milestones almost always involved adding an additional forty-five-pound plate to each side of the bar. Lifters, practicing their characteristic humility, referred to the amount of forty-five-pound plates on the bar by how many plates were on *one side* of the bar—such that when one squatted six plates, he was "squatting three plates"; and when he deadlifted eight plates, he was "deadlifting four plates"; and when, as Harold prepared to do now, he bench-pressed four plates, he was "benching two plates," and so on. These lifts were rites of passage, and no matter how many times Harold had lifted 225 pounds, it still felt like an accomplishment, and a reminder of his true identity—225 had been a struggle; now he could rep it out.

Harold felt subtly delighted as he retracted his shoulder blades against the bench, pinching them together on the leather, sliding his feet slightly back on the floor and pressing into the ground. He arched his back, wrapping his fingers around the bar. His arms quivered slightly as he unracked the bar and held it above his chest. The weight felt heavier than expected. Some days the weight felt heavier than others. Harold envisioned himself lifting the weight. He controlled the weight down to his chest—then pressed up.

Harold did three more reps, then reracked it.

Good.

Sitting up from underneath the bar, he felt reborn. Any lift that involved the possibility of being crushed to death meant that one had to adopt a sort of spiritual disposition toward it. One could not—would not—simply get under the weight without being propelled by some unseen force. And regardless of whether or not one found God, like Mel, or harnessed some kind of death wish, or heroic impulse, like Casey or Harold, one still had to descend into oneself and confront oneself there.

Harold waited two minutes exactly, glancing at the clock every few seconds, pacing back and forth and standing still, then slid back down onto the bench.

He readied himself, then descended.

The blinding white light inside the gym flashed black, and his vision became silver, as the bar cut through time and space; he lowered the bar and then pressed it up and away. The weight did not fall onto Harold's trachea and kill him; nor did it simply stick to his chest, causing him to call for help; no, he held the barbell up over himself again now; he let it down—then lifted.

There were many ways a lift could go wrong besides killing you. Only four or so people died each year from lifting. More often, you'd be afflicted with a minor tweak or strain, in the rotator cuff or some other tendon or joint, which hurt in such a way that it caused you to stop doing certain exercises for a period of time. Though injuries were often small and healed themselves, they still made everything miserable, because you could not simply get into the gym and go hard, instead becoming plagued by many *considerations*—always too aware of the position of the body, knowing that any minor shift could make the injury worse, and never feeling totally sure what might send a shooting pain through the afflicted area—such that your "minor" injury was always on your mind. Harold generally did his best to overcome, to adopt the proper mindset and go even harder with his unaffected lifts, but he often lacked the patience to let small things heal, and so instead of strategically resting for a short period, or focusing on other kinds of exercises, he lifted through the pain and made a small injury bigger over time. With lifters, everything grew. Muscles grew, resilience grew—but so did injuries, and these neurotic *considerations* . . .

As Harold stood, waiting for his next set, he looked around, avoiding eye contact with women, pacing in a small circle next to the bench. He stopped pacing and stood completely still, staring at himself in the mirror. Harold was full of living blood. He felt happier and more confident.

Harold pictured the employee with the cross necklace smiling and laughing at the high desk, and then remembered a passage he'd copied down from Mel's autobiography in his notes app. He searched "flesh" and found it.

God is the word made flesh. God is the word incarnate, the one True Word—flesh. In the beginning, there was the word—there was a typo here, "the wrd"—only God, only word. Then God made humanity in his image, but we became monsters. And so God sent his only son, and the word became flesh, so that we might come to know him. We could not sufficiently come to know a word. We could only come to know a flesh-word. The word alone did not work. Here again there was a typo, "wrk." *But when the word became flesh and dwelt among us we were saved. We were saved by the word which became flesh—not merely by the word, and not merely by the flesh, but by the word-flesh, or the flesh-word. God is not mere flesh, and he did not make mere flesh in us. But he is also not just a word. In the beginning was the word, and only later came the flesh; but in God's time, which is outside of time, there has always been this word-flesh; or, really, word-flesh-spirit.* Harold imagined the employee with the cross necklace approaching him from behind, catching him reading. *The spirit is the process that makes dead flesh come alive.*

He felt a strange pleasure, almost like being touched, when he pictured the employee hovering above him. Harold had only half read the text; much of his mind was occupied with imagining the employee behind him, reading over his shoulder.

Mel's autobiography was outlandishly over-wrought. But it was better than his biography. Mel's biographer was a Christian, and so was biased; he wrote about how, at the peak of Mel's career, Mel would ask God to help him "get out of his own way," so that it was just God and the weight, with no Mel in the middle. Mel "removed himself from the equation" so that, in his biographer's words, paraphrasing Mel, "it was God lifting the weight." Mel, one of the strongest men in the world, became plagued by self-doubt. Mel would strip down to his posing trunks and get oiled up and spray-tanned and his breathing would become percussive and he would forget how to breathe. Mel would be in the middle of a lift, and his knee would ache, or his wrist would wiggle, and thoughts about his own mortality would consume him, and he would imagine getting crumpled and folded over like a chair. After trying everything—different modes of therapy, even medication—Mel had been struck one day by a sculpture of Jesus, whose physique was so well proportioned, even while dying on a cross, that Mel decided to look into Christianity—and thus began a relatively quick conversion to the faith. Paradoxically, Mel's biographer wrote, loosely quoting Mel's own journal, Mel felt stronger when he relied on something outside of himself: the more he became aware of all the workings of his body, the more he became aware of its fallibility—how his body could break down or fail at any time, or how his mind could get in the way of his body's capabilities. Mel's body, despite being one of the strongest on Earth, could not quell his encroaching doom. He had to put his faith in something else.

Harold turned, half expecting to actually see the employee he was imagining, but not seeing him, and instead whipping his neck around only to make accidental eye contact with a menacing guy he'd never seen before. He looked away.

As Harold looked down, he imagined life as a road, unfurling unpredictably before him as he traveled—sometimes curving, sometimes turning—he wanted to become a person with an open-ended life, in which unexpected possibilities might materialize, and he wanted to adventurously embrace them—but when he was at Shepherd he felt as if he'd pulled off at some old roadside shack, inhabited by unwelcoming locals, and had decided to live there. Each day, Harold awoke with a dim sense of wonder—maybe today would be the day he'd leave the shack; perhaps a paragraph of one of his papers would unexpectedly go viral, and he'd be asked to speak on the news, where he could finally display his intelligence for the world, who would admire him; or maybe he'd receive a mysterious phone call that gave him directions to a faraway place, promising him some compellingly mysterious award upon arrival.

Instead, Harold's life felt like words inside a book: giving the illusion of narrative freedom, but in reality typeset and contained between two covers. Life, Harold thought—quoting Casey, following Schopenhauer—was a book that had already been written. One only had to read it.

Maybe every choice was an illusion. Even so, Harold wanted an experience of reality, not a mere representation of it. The clanging weights were a start. The clanging weights were *real*. He didn't want his body to be something he ignored, like a fact running counter to an academic's theory; he wanted his body to reflect something beyond it. Harold wanted his body to look and feel like a body, not a graveyard, or a word. And as he began this movement from airiness to physicality, from imagination to reality—from sky to ground in one sense, but from ground to sky in another—he learned that the body had its own dynamic characteristics. The body ached and screamed, but it also spoke and sang. The body had its own way of thinking. The body had its own words. Harold was beginning to learn the language of his body.

V

THE BLACK RUBBERY MAT BUBBLED UNPRE-
dictably beneath Harold's back as he held one sixty-
pound dumbbell in each hand, palms facing each other
above his chest—knees bent, feet firm—and moved
his arms out, then lowered them, slow and controlled.
He felt his chest stretch. He fought gravity. Harold
raised the dumbbells up toward each other again, consciously contracting his chest throughout the entire
movement, and squeezing as hard as he could at the
top. He imagined his muscle fibers microscopically
tearing, cells shooting through his body toward his
chest like electrical currents, or little guppies rushing
in a river—blood.

This was the secret to growing muscle: the mind.
When most people lift something, their goal is to get
from point A to point B: a box is on the floor and you

want it on the table and so you move it from the floor to the table. Simple. Most new lifters carry this lay-men's conception of lifting over into the gym. People move around crudely, without paying attention, like zombies, or dogs. They press the barbell up above their chest or up over their head or curl it up, then lower it—all the while only dimly aware of the beginning and the end.

But the beginning and the end were unimportant. It was the middle that mattered. Harold experienced the middle of the movement. He resisted the crass dichotomy of here and there, the gross binary of rest-ing and flexing: Harold entered fully into the entire process. He felt his muscles stretch and strain. He felt them tear. He involved himself directly, not only in the beginning and the end but *in the middle*. The middle was the hardest place to be. The middle was the part nobody thought about. When young people imagined their lives, they thought of themselves as young, then old. It was impossible for a young person to imagine himself at forty-three. Or fifty. It was the same with novice lifters. One could understand the beginning and the end of a lift, but the middle remained funda-mentally mysterious.

It's hard to feel the middle of a movement. It's hard to use the proper muscles. Often, one uses his shoul-ders instead of his pectorals, or his glutes instead of his quads, or his hips instead of his biceps, and ruins everything. One uses his back and ruins everything, or uses his traps and ruins everything. The impor-tant thing was to connect one's mind with the specific muscle being worked—and in order to do that, one needed to enter into the muscle.

Harold entered into the muscle. He shrunk himself down into nothing. He confronted the nothingness. He lived in the dark night of nothingness until his whole being became blood rushing into his muscles. His consciousness became another molecule, a cell among cells, and by the time the weight was lifted to the top position, he was literally inside himself, burning and firing and pumped-up alive. Consciousness was not a machine, or a mistake, but an ever-present awareness of the obstacle; Harold existed in relation to the obstacle—he was not static being but becoming, overcoming—and during the process Harold's entire identity felt aligned. He was one with the pump. He was blood.

The new lifter, when he just starts out, is unfamiliar with his body. He doesn't know how to communicate with it. He doesn't know how to hear his body talk. He doesn't know how to respond. Most people aren't aware of their bodies unless they are experiencing pain or pleasure. Most people think lifting the weights is the hard part. It's not.

On YouTube, where Harold learned everything about lifting that he hadn't learned from Casey, people would mention "squeezing at the top" of a motion, "controlling the weight the whole time," and "making sure you really feel it," and Harold assumed that, because he was lifting the weights, he was doing all of this. It is easy to assume that we are doing something well, when in reality we are just doing something, and in the end not really doing it at all. One thinks that he is *squeezing at the top*, or *controlling the weight the whole time*, or *making sure he really feels it*, when in reality he is bungling something fundamentally foreign to him, deludedly moving from point A to point B, unaware.

Harold's YouTube algorithm had started promoting only fitness videos, which he'd taken to watching indiscriminately while bored: he'd spend evenings watching videos about people who were suspected of lying about taking steroids, lifting montages, "What I Eat in a Day" videos, and instructional videos—such as the one that illuminated the sad fact of Harold's lack of mind-muscle connection—like "Can't Get Big Biceps? Just Do THIS!!!"

"Can't Get Big Biceps? Just Do THIS!!!" began with instructions: put your arm at your side, then bend it to a ninety-degree angle and flex your bicep as hard as you can. The guy in the video asked if the viewer "felt any discomfort." Harold did not. He then said to lift your arm a little more, supinate your wrist, and squeeze. "If you don't feel any discomfort now," he said, "we have a problem."

They had a problem. Harold didn't feel any discomfort. When the guy in the video, whom Harold had begun to resent a little, told Harold to lift his arm out to the side, so that his arms were perpendicular to the floor and his elbow was in line with his shoulder, and squeeze, Harold felt hopeful. Surely Harold would be able to experience discomfort here.

But Harold didn't feel any discomfort. He was screwed.

One way to develop mind-muscle connection, the video explained, was to move light dumbbells into each position Harold had just gone through, moving one's arms slightly so that blood began to pump into the bicep. "Discomfort," the man in the video said. "That is the feeling you want every time."

Easy enough, Harold thought. He resolved to get in the habit of practicing mind-muscle connection, starting the very next day.

But he did not start doing it regularly; nor did he start the very next day. For months, Harold was only distantly aware of the fact that he was not "feeling" his biceps contracting during curls, and, though he could occasionally feel his right bicep contract—barely, and only when his arm was at certain angles—he almost never felt his left. Still, he didn't incorporate any of the video's suggestions into his routine. He'd watched the video, felt convinced by the video, and even resolved to do what the video suggested—he just didn't do it.

This was the kind of superior knowledge that lifting provided. One could know about mind-muscle connection, indeed even *believe* in mind-muscle connection (which is to say one could have mind-muscle connection swirling around in one's head like a broken, endlessly flushing toilet); and he could make flailing, haphazard attempts at practicing mind-muscle connection, feeling vaguely pained by his new knowledge, meekly curling his arms, once or twice, at random times; but in the end, he was confronted with his own lack of discipline, a kind of anti-learning inside himself that did not want to grow. In short, "Can't Get Big Biceps? Just Do THIS!!!" taught Harold about mind-muscle connection, but it also taught him about the conflicted nature of the will. Harold could not simply flush his new thoughts in his toilet head and expect his muscles to grow: with lifting, knowledge had to be applied—it had to work.

In the undulating Lawes halls, nothing had to work. Ideas were never tested against the cold fact of reality, never held to any kind of standard. In most endeavors, there was a point at which an idea came in contact with reality, and if the idea wasn't harmonious with reality, one was forced to reevaluate. One day, passing the science building, which had been converted from an old cathedral, Harold felt a camaraderie he'd never felt before, viewing himself in that moment as a scientist: the gym was a laboratory, where one conducted experiments on one's body and mind, and achieved visible results; in science, as in the gym, there was a measure. In Lawes—in the life of pure language—there was no such measure, and, therefore, nothing to prevent nonsense from spiraling down uninterrupted forever.

In theory, however, Harold thought, literature was actually *more like* lifting than the hard sciences and other disciplines. While so many flimsy philosophies and theories were doomed to die by their own dogma, endlessly ascending stacks of even more dogma, climbing up and up, only to realize, too late, as they're falling into the abyss, that the dogmas that the current dogmas were stacked on were unstable and rickety, literature could stand outside this mess and shed light on it, through narrative. Narrative was one antidote to scattered, unruly ideas, Harold knew; integrated knowledge, manifested as action, was another. Action was a kind of narrative.

In theory, whereas certain disciplines were made up of information, often in the context of a very narrow narrative, literature could serve some much-needed aesthetic function. Among other things, literature could integrate information in more dynamic ways than other mediums allowed. It was one thing for a philosophy professor to say *morality is absolute* (which no philosophy professor at Shepherd College would say), and another to read *Crime and Punishment* and to experience what Raskolnikov experiences, to *be* Raskolnikov, in some sense; and to *go through the Raskolnikov process*, and become convinced not that *morality is absolute*, as an old philosophy professor might so crassly put it, but that *Raskolnikov is a Napoleon-esque figure, as am I, squished into dementedness by the conditions of the present age.* One read *Crime and Punishment* and came to know something about the structure of society and one's own place within it; one listened to a philosophy professor and got the sense that there were no real stakes at all; that the true end of thinking was just more thinking, a mental exercise, mere syllogisms and dogmas—death.

That was what lay at the end of all philosophy: syllogisms and dogmas. Not one syllogism and one dogma but many syllogisms and many dogmas, and more syllogisms and more dogmas on top of those. Literature, like lifting, was the synthesis of action and reflection. This was what made it worth pursuing. However, most literary types did not act or reflect but rather brutalized and evaded: their action was inaction and their reflection was avoidance. There was no risk, and no reward. Literature was closer to the process of integrating knowledge—of taking something *known* and making it *actually known*—than any other humanities discipline. In short, literature had potential because literature was closer to lifting.

Of course, in practice, literature was nothing like lifting, and it was nothing like computer science or engineering, and it was nothing like action or integrated knowledge, and it was exactly like every other humanities discipline, with the exception that it was possibly even more confused and deluded than all of them.

Harold pressed his shoulder blades against the inclined bench and pressed the dumbbells up, then squeezed his chest at the top and exhaled, almost grunted, feeling his pecs press up, pulled tight beneath his skin. On the eighth rep, he held the dumbbells with his elbows slightly above ninety degrees, applying maximum tension to the muscle, until his chest was screaming.

Harold flexed his pecs and looked at himself in the mirror. He took his eyes off the mirror and paced back and forth. His body throbbed. He flexed his pecs until it felt like fiery pins were needling their way up from his muscles and out through his skin; he grimaced and let out an *ahhh*, then reeled himself in; he unflexed his pecs and let the muscles—now thick with blood—soften and sink, like dense Jell-O cupped in sacks of stretched flesh. He twisted his face into knots—then let it fall.

Now came the best part: the real reason Harold came to the gym in the first place. Harold experienced a sensation he thought of as "opening up." He received new eyes. When blood flows into your muscles, it changes your eyes. The sensation starts in your blood and stretches out over the whole world, through your eyes. It's as if each color contains a deeper, richer layer of itself, invisible during the rote machinery of life—grading papers, opening laptop—which gets revealed only when blood makes muscle thick and full. Before, Harold saw colors, but now he could actually see; before, Harold was breathing, but now he *could actually breathe.* Everything opened into a new and wondrous layer of itself, such that it remained the same, but different.

Now when Harold looked at himself in the mirror, he did not feel the usual self-consciousness: he did not notice his hairline or the fact that he needed to shave. When he noticed something undesirable—for example, that his left arm was smaller than his right and that his left shoulder hung down a little lower, so that he appeared slightly crooked—he perceived it with an eye toward fixing it: his arm size disparity became something to work on as opposed to something dumbly wrong; his crookedness became the opportunity to straighten up. Even these things only flitted through Harold's mind; for the most part, Harold was not thinking about anything except his pecs: squeezing them, stretching them, relaxing them. He was in the zone. He had a pump.

Montaigne thought that each body part had a mind of its own. Harold greedily extrapolated: each individual muscle was a brain. On a strong man, what at first appeared to be bulging pectorals were in reality two bulging brains. Biceps were brains; triceps were brains; even abs, which at first appeared to be vaguely rectangular muscles, were in fact vaguely rectangular brains. This was why getting a pump made Harold euphoric: one's mood was not determined by the thinking part of the brain in one's head but by the active part of the brains in one's muscles. The gut is a brain. The sexual organs are brains. And muscles are brains. The head-brain is the only brain that is not a real brain—but an adversary.

So Harold loved the pump. When muscles become engorged, one's whole being becomes engorged; one's soul becomes engorged; everything pulsates—and everything appears new. All throughout human history, people were getting pumps. They were fighting wars or picking food or chopping wood and getting pumps. Now people were devoid of the pump. People were pump-devoid. Modern people lived motionless lives: hunched over laptops, phones, tablets. Their bodies wanted the pump, were literally dying for the pump, but people could not listen to their bodies, because they did not speak their body's language. In our modern world, Harold thought, where each individual part is separated out and accounted for, the pump must be discovered, or discerned.

People search for the pump in drugs, in sex, in places of worship. They search for it in books. But the only place where they can truly find it is inside themselves. Imagine a pump, Harold thought, standing next to the bench, that exists outside oneself—an *external pump*—it is a flagrant contradiction, a farce!

When you lift, the muscles tear and the blood rushes into the muscle; the plasma gets trapped in the spaces between cells, and the muscle becomes engorged. A beginner will experience this strange new sensation as pain (it is painful; your muscles are ripping), but after a while it starts to feel good.

In Harold's favorite documentary, a famous bodybuilder described the pump in a quote Harold had memorized: "I am, like, getting the feeling of cumming in the gym," the bodybuilder said, smiling. "I'm getting the feeling of cumming at home; I'm getting the feeling of cumming backstage; when I pump up, when I pose out in front of five thousand people, I get the same feeling, so I am cumming day and night. It's terrific, right? So you know, I am in heaven."

However, Harold considered over the years, this bodybuilder got it exactly backward: an orgasm feels like the pump, not the other way around. The pump is far superior to an orgasm; an orgasm is a pump derivative. The post-pump tiredness is substantively different than after an orgasm. One is the satisfaction of hard work, which helps nourish and strengthen the body, and therefore the soul, in all aspects; the other is a depletion, a suck. Casey was the one who originally enlightened Harold on this esoteric truth. "If there is any good feeling after doing the deed," he told Harold one day, stopping beneath an oak tree during one of their walks on campus, "it is a result of the hip thrusts, or holding oneself up in a plank position; the minor pump one might achieve . . ." Harold watched Dolly pass behind Casey, and tried to discern whether or not she'd heard him. "Pay attention to the way you feel after you indulge yourself," Casey said. "Not immediately after, but thirty minutes after, an hour after. Pay attention to the way you feel later that day. Pay attention to your energy when you wake up the next morning. If you are not messing your life up in some other way, to skew the experiment, you will see what I mean." He paused. "Then try not orgasming for a month." He continued, "You might even find some literary value in the irony . . . Cumming, despite or perhaps because of the fact that it creates life, when spurted incoherently to no real end, creates a kind of death inside the cummer, it is a deathly act . . ." He patted Harold on the back, and smiled generously.

Harold picked up the dumbbells and sat back down on the bench for his next set. On the eighth rep, when he did the isometric hold, it began burning after five seconds, but he dug his heels into the ground—he imagined pushing the floor down with his feet, crashing through the floor beneath, down into the center of the Earth—and mentally resolved to hold the weights for twenty seconds. It was harder for Harold to endure a slow, steady burn than the acute strain of heavy sets. He counted slowly—then quickly. His left arm started jiggling. He groaned. He thought about dropping the weights. He imagined onlookers watching. He would not drop the weights. After fifteen seconds, his legs started jiggling too, and he whimpered.

Ffff. Yes. Fffff. Eh—Harold oscillated between thinking about dropping the weight and resolving to push through.

Harold dropped the weights, having completed twenty seconds. Rrrrr, he thought. Harold recalled something Casey had said . . . or almost recalled it . . . The memory floated in and out of him like an impression. Casey spoke with authority, and Harold felt almost in awe of him: the unexpected things he said, the gentle, firm way in which he guided Harold through workouts; when Casey lifted with Harold, he felt receptive, and honored, like a door had been open to a whole new world that was previously inaccessible to him.

By some strange alchemy, Harold constructed a memory of Casey saying something that was really Harold's own thoughts, and Harold imagined—as he did in the meeting room—that he was preparing for a nonexistent podcast, this time about a nonexistent essay he'd written about lifting. There is a lot of anti-lifter propaganda in the media, and, fundamentally, inside of us, he thought-talked, imagining that he was remembering something Casey had said, which festers in the dank parts of our being, and which promotes ugliness and seeks to produce ugliness in all things. It is the frumpy mother in our unconscious, which seeks to expand outward, subsuming all hard lines into itself, erasing boundaries, borders, distinctions, all hierarchies, all individuality and beauty, everything *distinct*, until all that is left is the tyrannical flesh of the frumpified: smothering, chaotic, formless matter; a stifling, asphyxiating blanket, suffocating everything that could have been or tried to be. Harold pressed the dumbbells up above his chest and squeezed; he was feeling uncharacteristically articulate and confident; his thoughts, which he continued to think in Casey's voice, were punctuated with heavy, short breaths. From an undifferentiated psychic swamp, he thought-talked as Casey, we've emerged into blossoming consciousness, over and against the forces of undifferentiation and confusion, the anti-consciousness of slovenly bodies. This is what bodybuilders build their bodies up against: the frumpification of consciousness itself. People are confused about bodybuilders' relationship to pain, because most people are possessed by the false promise of comfort. They sit on their couches for so long that they sink into their couches and in the end they *become* couches: their heads become couches, their brains become couches, their legs become couches.

Harold held the dumbbells just above ninety degrees.

Fleeing pain, he thought, forgetting to count, we have practiced our couch art and have turned into couches: but we are in fact less comfortable than ever, because as we retreat into couch-consciousness, reality itself weighs down on us, and so we become increasingly squished and oppressed. In the end, despite our couch-transformation attempt, which is really our couch sorcery, pain is inevitable—and it becomes ever more painful the more avoidant we are.

Lifters—gah—know this, Harold thought, imitating Casey, still holding the weight up; it is not the pain—rrr—but the quality of the pain that matters. Harold dropped the weights. He stood and paced. The pain the day after a good workout, Harold thought-talked, is contained to oneself; then it produces strength and beauty, which lifters model for others in an aspirational way. The pain during lifting, he thought-talked, and afterward when you're sore, is like growing pains—there is something better on the other side. But the pain after a day of self-centered degeneracy spreads out into the world, negatively affecting countless others, spreading pain and more pain exponentially. Some pain results from tragedy, which one must accept; but a lot of pain is chosen. There are things we can't control and things we can control, and most of what causes true pain falls into the latter category. Pain—the sustained kind of pain that really bothers people—is always a choice.

And so the pump does not enter into a painless world to introduce pain, Harold thought-talked, but rather it enters a world rife with pain and creates the kind of pain that *produces growth*. We experience and cause pain despite our best efforts. It is the *kind of* pain we experience and produce—as well as our reaction to pain imposed on us—that differentiates the weak from the strong. Harold carried his dumbbells back to the rack. When he went to set them down, there were thirty-five-pound weights in the slot where his sixty-pound weights were supposed to go; he looked at the thirty-five-pound slot, but there were thirty-pound weights in there. Harold looked for any open slots, worrying momentarily that David had come to the gym and played a prank on him, and dropped his weights in the first place he found an opening.

Many people don't even know that they produce pain, he thought-talked. They view themselves as essentially good, and they view others as essentially bad. In short, they view themselves as victims, and others as victimizers. The lifter embodies both. He inflicts pain, but he inflicts pain on himself, so he also receives pain; he is both victim and victimizer; he is the complete human being unto himself.

Of course, he continued in Casey's voice, most lifters are not complete human beings, and are significantly deformed in one way or another. He imagined the woman who stood at the tall desk with the Hill's employees as the podcast host now, fawning over him. One can find them in gyms all over the world, totally missing the point. The powerlifters, with their ogreish physiques and fetish for only three lifts, are really glorified cavemen, he thought-talked, and the bodybuilders, who all have body dysmorphia, are constantly fussing with this or that accessory, grotesquely proportional, ridiculously finicky. And then there are the random psychos, who populate the gym like roaches, aimless and skittering, and who will remain weak forever . . .

Behind the benches, a white man in a black tank top and a backward flat-brimmed hat performed curls. He looked like the front man of a rap-rock band, tribal tattoos twisting up his right arm; he hoisted the dumbbells up with his hips, even bending at the knees a little before lifting, essentially humping the weight up. He looked like an inflamed skin tag. He was big and pimply and clearly on steroids. When people thought of steroids, they imagined perfectly chiseled physiques, but the truth, Harold learned, was that most roiders had only decent physiques, and sometimes even bad physiques. This backward-hatted wart was one such roider. Harold felt repulsed, and was overcome with a feeling of intuitive sympathy for the roider's wife.

Nearby, a thin white kid also did curls, wearing a beanie and over-ear headphones. Harold could tell instantly and with 100 percent certainty that he was evil. Often, it was not the strongest but the weakest who were the most cruel. The kid's head accessories, in addition to the fact that he was making a "sexy face" in the mirror—leaning his head forward and angling it to inspect his jawline, while looking directly into his own eyes, and curling one side of his upper lip—betrayed a terrifying inner life. He had undoubtedly been bullied, Harold thought, and had undoubtedly deserved it. He looked like he'd be fun to bully. He was probably sixteen. The kid had likely harbored fantasies of being a bully himself. Often, it is not getting bullied but rather the fact that others *see* you getting bullied that is the most humiliating. In the end, the bullied kid dreams only of revenge; daily humiliations simmer in him like a stew, and since he cannot act in the face of his oppressor, or become a bully himself, he retreats into fantasy, then takes his hatred out on some other, smaller victim—like an animal. As Harold watched the beanie-wearing child do curls, he pictured him torturing a kitten. Harold wanted to go up to him and tell him that no matter how many curls he did, he would never avenge himself . . . that he would never get tenure, or—

Harold smirked. Never get *better*, he corrected himself. Harold looked down, removing his eyes from the mirror.

Two young women in spandex shorts walked and stopped at the bench next to Harold. Ff. Fffggg.

Harold's eyes, operating independently, tried to trick him by rising toward the mirror and looking at himself, but they instantly drifted toward the girls— he looked at the floor.

Harold, despite glancing in the mirror repeatedly, each time whipped his neck back around and down, or stared with a focused expression at himself. There had recently been a string of videos going around online of women filming themselves at the gym, "catching" men looking at them, with voice-overs, or text on the screen, describing the "harassment" they were experiencing. Words like "creep" and "pervert," camera zoomed in on the guy's face, who was often only ambiguously looking in the woman's direction, and even then only for no longer than a few seconds at a time. It would be horrible, Harold thought, to accidentally get caught gawking in a video like that. What would happen to his job? His reputation?

In one recent video, which amassed almost six hundred thousand views, a man approached a woman and asked her how many sets she had left—a common enough occurrence in a crowded gym. But the woman stood and started yelling at the man, "I'm sick of coming to the gym to try to *improve myself*, minding my own *business*, and men like you make me feel like I'm about to get *kidnapped*." The girl's head swiveled slightly and her eyes glanced back to see the angle in her phone; she backed up until her butt took up most of the frame. There was some indiscriminate, apologetic murmuring; then her voice cut through: "Then don't act like a *kidnapper*!"

The responses online were overwhelmingly negative toward the girl, but that was just what Harold saw on his feed: every time something elicited a strong reaction from the corner of the internet he spent time on, he assumed there was an equal and opposite reaction that he wasn't aware of. If he ever appeared in a video like that, he knew, his colleagues and the student body would not take his side. Harold glanced at the area surrounding the girls near him, in search of a covertly hidden phone.

He lay back on the bench. As his chest started to burn, he looked at himself in the mirror, but then his gaze shifted toward the girls, so he stopped looking in the mirror; he tried to motivate himself by telling himself that the burn would blow his chest up, and if his chest blew up, then girls like those next to him—clean, young, well adjusted—would find him more attractive; but the instant he considered the girls' attraction toward him, he dropped the weights.

Harold sat up, trying to keep his eyes on the floor.

But he immediately looked at the girls in the mirror. He looked away; he could feel their presence next to him; he couldn't make himself forget. His eyes flickered up into the mirror and he accidentally made eye contact with one of them.

Ffff—gghh. He should not have looked away; he was always looking away; he never held eye contact with girls in the gym. He was never sure how his face looked, and he didn't want to accidentally appear like a psycho. But that was a risk he had to be willing to take: now he seemed weak, cowardly, avoidant. Harold wanted to hold someone's eyes. One day, he would hold Vance's eyes, and the girls' eyes . . . He would hold everyone's eyes and experience the thrill of human connection.

Harold accidentally made eye contact with the same girl in the mirror again. He looked away. Ffff. He felt his heart beating; they were only one bench apart; a part of him wondered if she could "feel" his heartbeat, if she could feel his eyes through the mirror, or feel his thoughts; he tried to breathe into his thoughts; he felt sick.

Harold picked up the dumbbells. Real men did not lift for women, he reminded himself. This was another thing one learned after going to the gym for some time: women did not like big muscles. *Men* liked big muscles. Men lifted for other men.

Harold performed his last set of incline flies, mind flitting back and forth like an injured bat. When he stood, he shook his arms out, returned the dumbbells to the rack, then scurried away from the girls.

Good riddance . . . he thought, walking with his back to the women. Now I will not be in your way . . .

Harold walked toward the water fountain, before remembering that his next exercise was actually in the same area he'd just come from. Ffff; he'd been coming to this gym for years, and running this program for months, how could he make such an absent-minded mistake? If he went back the way he came, the girls might notice. Of course, they probably wouldn't notice at all . . . He could just get a sip of water, so that it seemed as though he'd come over here intentionally?

No, he thought. They cannot make me drink. But suddenly, he was thirsty . . .

Instead of going back the way he came, he passed through another area and entered the bench portion of the gym from the opposite side he'd left it.

As he walked through the area with various machines, he passed a man who was talking to himself. The man was doing shrugs on the shrug machine, yelling "Yep" and "Alright," interspersed with grunts, and when he finished his set, he continued.

"You mmmm, yeah motherf—alright—yeah, yeah." He paced purposefully and spoke in a sinister, self-contained tone. "M—yeah—motherfu—" He growled. He was older, mid-fifties or early sixties. His large, roping veins snaked up his entire body. "I'm gonna kill you."

VI

HAROLD FINISHED HIS CHEST EXERCISES, then tricep exercises, as if in a daze; his thoughts became a dull buzz; the light shone warmly through the floor-to-ceiling windows; Harold felt expansive, wordless gratitude.

He remembered, with a tinge of nostalgia, the first poem he'd ever published in an online literary journal, when he was sixteen.

> *And still the light*
> *Pours down; men laud the day*
> *I shun the sun and cast my soul*
> *Into the shadowy pit.*

Harold looked out the window until it was time to perform his last set. He picked up the weights . . .

He reracked them . . . He thought of getting a quick ab pump, mainly just to feel them fill with blood. The core was important—everything stemmed from the legs and the core. One could get away with not having a solid foundation for a time, but it would always cause problems eventually. He stopped at the pull-up bar on the way back to the locker room and did two sets of hanging leg raises. The lower portion of his stomach felt like it was being gripped by many hot fingers. He looked around the gym one last time. He started walking.

VII

━━

THE DENSE WOOD FILLED HAROLD'S NOSTRILS
as his lungs labored to adjust to the new pressure. He
sank into the dark room where nothing existed but
body and heat. The simmering sensation on his skin
felt like a pill when it kicked in: something entered
into his body and rose up within him. Harold nodded
at the men in the sauna—two amateur bodybuilders
named Darrell and Mike, and a small, well-built Asian
man Harold didn't recognize—as he stepped up to the
second level, where it was hottest, and sat.

One towel was wrapped around Harold's waist,
and another was draped across his shoulders, so that,
when he leaned back, his skin didn't make direct contact with the sauna wall. He'd developed minor back
acne recently, and he didn't want to aggravate it.

Puddles of sweat pooled beneath Darrell and

Mike. The Asian man sat silently in the corner, look-ing intently at the ground.

The Asian man was much smaller than Darrell and Mike, and this, coupled with his silence compared to to the others' loud, argumentative voices, made him seem particularly meek.

The bodies before him sat in stark contrast to his colleagues' bodies, which sagged and slouched, lop-sidedly lumped or juttingly boned beneath ill-fitting button-ups and pantsuits. The physiques here were chiseled, intentional—glistening.

Harold's heartbeat slowed, diffusing through his body and into his head. His muscles weren't brains now, as Montaigne wrote, but hearts. His blood be-came thick; his skin tingled. He leaned back and closed his eyes. "You're missing the point," Mike said. His voice was nasal, yet measured and reserved. "The tricep makes up *two-thirds* of the arm. So you should train your triceps two-thirds more than your biceps."

"And?" Darrell said.

Harold untangled his headphones. He could al-ready feel them getting warm, but he would have ten to fifteen minutes before he'd have to leave because the plastic got too hot in his ears, or his phone overheated.

Harold navigated to YouTube on his phone in the amber-hued semidarkness, and tapped the first video that the algorithm recommended, "The Greatest Bodybuilding FEUD You Didn't Know About."

An ad for a virtual therapy service appeared on the small screen. Garish, twinkling music simmered into Harold's ears, over a video of a woman brushing her teeth while walking around her apartment, as he looked up and saw the Asian man staring straight ahead, despondently.

Darrell flexed his pecs and smiled.

Harold communed with the dense air. He drank it. He sighed.

Mike cleared his throat as Harold tried to steal some longer glimpses of his body. Harold had always admired Mike's body, which blossomed up impressively: his massive lats, slabs of dense muscle, looked like an inverted triangle, or wings. If he weren't so heavy, Harold thought, Mike would be able to simply flex his lats and wait for the wind to pick him up and carry him away. He had boulder-esque delts; his quads and hamstrings thickened out beneath his thin and rippled waist. These proportions, on a person as opposed to an inanimate object, like stone, seemed somehow impossible, even as Harold was staring at them in the flesh. Mike was intimidating not because of his size but because of his *symmetry*.

Often, we are attracted not to the most beautiful person but to the most beautiful person up to a point, past which we are repulsed. This repulsion comes from the fact that too much beauty—like divinity— contains an element of horror. A man, encountering a woman who is too beautiful, feels no sexual desire, only a chilly distance; a woman, encountering a man who is too muscular, feels disgusted. Of course, the proper response to this kind of beauty was awe. One did not feel attracted to it exactly, but reverent in the presence of it, and called almost to worship it.

Despite his physique, Mike sounded like a total nerd. Harold grimaced at his grating tone in the moment of silence between when the YouTube ad ended and the video began, during which he could hear Mike say "improper fo—" The video began with a swirling graphic of the YouTube channel's logo: a barbell with the text FREAK STRENGTH.

"Alright, guys, welcome back to the channel," the narration began. "Here again with another *sweet* bodybuilding video. This time from the golden age . . ." The voice sounded like it had been recorded straight into the laptop mic; the video so far was just a series of black-and-white images of famous bodybuilders, rapidly appearing on the screen, like a PowerPoint.

Maybe I could start a lifting channel, Harold considered as the heat pressed in on him invisibly and he felt microscopic beads forming in his pores. English *Lift*, he thought, considering a name for his imaginary channel, English . . . *Lift*erature . . . Welcome back . . .

Harold adjusted his phone to make sure no one could see the screen. If Darrell and Mike knew what Harold was watching, they'd try to have a conversation with him about it, and Harold wasn't in the mood. He leaned his head against the wall, peering down at the video over his nose.

Despite the title of the video—"The Greatest Bodybuilding FEUD You Didn't Know About"— which confidently asserted that Harold would not know about the feud in question, Harold did in fact already know about it: the video gave a little backstory, then summarized a popular story about Arnold

Schwarzenegger trying to sabotage Lou Ferrigno at the 1975 Mr. Olympia bodybuilding contest by giving him improper training advice and "getting in his head" before the posedown.

Harold remembered a book he'd read by Mike Mentzer, a legendary bodybuilder with an idiosyncratic training style, who viewed bodybuilding as a way to promote Ayn Rand's philosophy, and who wrote disparagingly about Schwarzenegger. Harold's earbuds began to heat up even more; plastic heated up at twice or three times the rate of Harold's skin, which he always wished would heat up more quickly: his flesh's resting temperature had always seemed "colder" than that of others, who had no problem sweating instantaneously in the sauna, whereas Harold always had to wait. Half memories of Mentzer's book emerged in Harold's mind at the same moment that the video began to play a slideshow of images of Mentzer.

"Arnold wanted to be better than the people he was competing against," the video said, "but Mike Mentzer wanted to raise the standard of bodybuilding itself. He was angry that Arnold would stoop so low as to sabotage others. Mike wanted to raise people up."

"Nooooo," Harold heard Darrell yell a few feet away. His syllables thickened in the background of the tinny audio in Harold's headphones.

"Mike believed," the video said, in a tone that reminded Harold of Mike Mentzer himself—in addition to, Harold realized, Mike's tone in the sauna—"in objective reality. He believed that man was meant to be a hero. He had a rationalist approach to bodybuilding, and to life in general."

"Oh God," Darrell said, at the exact moment Harold thought it.

The heat slowed Harold's brain but quickened his breath. Had Darrell actually spoken, or had Harold merely thought it? Had Darrell heard the video? No. It was impossible.

"For Mentzer, it was man's *rationality* that separated him from animals."

Harold glanced away from his phone, laboring to breathe, and saw Darrell hold up his pointer finger and thumb, rather dramatically, and curl them in toward each other like pincers. He shot his hand down to his thigh and began pinching himself.

"Man is fundamentally rational," the video went on. "Which is obvious if you think about it."

Darrell pinched his thigh. His tricep flexed so hard it began to shake. He grimaced.

"Mentzer had a posing philosophy that he called HUNGER," the video said. But Harold wasn't watching the video or paying attention. He already knew about HUNGER, which stood for "Height, Uplift, Nobility, Grandeur, Exaltation, and Reverence," and he remembered it distantly as the video described it, and he covertly observed Darrell and Mike, while simultaneously experiencing some unarticulated trepidation about his new imaginary YouTube channel.

Darrell gripped his wrist with his free hand, as if to generate more power, still pinching his thigh. Mike swung his giant legs, his quadriceps jiggling like gelatinous slabs. A dark shadow passed over Darrell's face as he furrowed his brow and focused on pinching himself. Darrell smiled, stopped pinching, and patted Mike on the back.

Mike fidgeted a little in reaction to the slap, and, as he turned, Harold saw blood, dripping down with the sweat. "Darrell, I don't expect," Harold read on Mike's lips—but he couldn't make out the rest.

"Bodybuilding was not just a philosophy for Mentzer," the video continued, "it was higher than philosophy, because it could integrate man's highest ideals, both intellectually and physically, in the abstract and concrete."

Harold's headphones began to create a pinching sensation in his ears as his body relaxed and the occasional bead of sweat dripped from his wrist and chest. He wished Casey were there . . .

Darrell laughed, then paused, looking at Mike's body. Harold heard the words "fullness" and "back" as Darrell patted Mike wetly again.

Harold noticed that Darrell's thigh had been cut open. He was bleeding.

Mike flexed his pecs, and small droplets of sweat jumped off his body, as though he had been flicked.

Darrell now appeared less friendly. He dropped some spit from his mouth down into the growing pool of sweat between his feet. His toes were crooked and spread unnaturally far apart. He spit again—this time into his new thigh wound. No one else seemed to notice that he was bleeding.

Harold closed his eyes. Both the video and the

voices around him sunk down into a part of him where they simmered semiconsciously. He imagined he was narrating a video for his new YouTube channel about Mike Mentzer's and Arnold Schwarzenegger's competing philosophies, trying to focus and thinking Rrrr... and Ma... when he heard Mike's and Darrell's voices get louder, cutting through the heavy heat.

The tension in the sauna seemed to paradoxically decrease as Mike and Darrell's conversation became more overtly confrontational. The sweat had finally started beading on Harold's skin and dripping down. He could taste it on the corners of his lips. His body was buzzing; his mind felt calmer than it had all day. It was as if Harold's thoughts were leaving him through his sweat, or as if the heat, entering him through his skin, then enveloped his thoughts. In short, Harold felt warm. But as soon as he acknowledged how comfortable he was, a screeching awareness of his proximity to others disrupted it. Until then, Harold had felt as if he'd been in another, mysterious world, where the rules of social engagement didn't apply; where Harold could stare openly at another man's muscles and not feel the need to look away or even speak to him; where he could watch a YouTube video mere feet from three other men and pretend he was alone. Now, however, Harold's small amount of self-reflection made him painfully aware of his predicament. Why had he brought his headphones into the sauna? He could have just been normal and quiet, like the Asian man, or congenial like Darrell and Mike...

Perhaps he'd brought his phone and headphones

in because he privately hoped Casey would text him, or even that Casey would join him in the sauna, appearing like some apparition. Or maybe, dimly recognizing that none of this would happen, Harold had essentially "pouted" by bringing in his phone and headphones, as if to send a message to those around him: Harold wanted Casey or no one at all.

A minute or so passed as Harold's thoughts, the video, and the voices outside him merged into an ambiguous unity, the distinctions among them compressed in the heat, which squeezed and shaped them together in a bustling clump of consciousness and flesh: Harold wanted to speak, but his thoughts kept merging with what he could hear of Darrell's and Mike's voices, and the video, so that he was never sure if what he wanted to contribute to the conversation had been something one of them had just said moments prior, something the video had said, or an authentic thought.

Without Harold noticing, the video had ended—or perhaps he'd accidentally pressed a button that caused the next video to play—and another began. Harold had instinctively turned the volume down on his phone, so as not to risk the others hearing it. There was nothing more annoying than when someone in the sauna was listening to something in headphones so loudly that anyone nearby could hear it. When Harold tapped the screen with his finger to reveal the title of the new video, the phone moved slower than usual, as if the internet itself was part of the sauna, or Harold's mind, and the title of the video appeared gradually like sand through a sieve, "Why LIBERTARIANISM is CUCKED F'sho!!"

Harold turned the volume on his phone down even more.

WHEN THE ASIAN man finally spoke, the whole room changed. For a moment, the mass of air was punctuated by something new, but the shift was short-lived, and his voice was quickly subsumed into the sauna, and things continued as before.

The Asian man had great proportions, everything was tight and lean, but he was tiny compared to Mike and Darrell, likely one hundred pounds lighter, if not more, and much shorter. He had an attractive, albeit severe, face. When he spoke, his square jaw tightened and he cut a stunningly dramatic figure, but the moment he stopped, his face softened, as if something had passed over him, then left him just as quickly.

"Mike," the Asian man said, then paused. The video was now playing clips of someone talking about Yukio Mishima, the Japanese novelist, with images of Mishima interspersed. This created an uncanny sensation in Harold: first the video Mike Mentzer mixed with Mike in the sauna; now Mishima mixed with the Asian man. People often feared that their phones "heard" them—someone would mention something out loud and then start getting ads for it—but now Harold half wondered if his phone could also "see," or if some mysterious invisible algorithm in his real life was entering into his phone. Harold's eyes buzzed.

"The Enlightenment has led to a degenerate society," the man in the video said. "John Stuart Mill, who some call the founder of liberalism, wrote about what he called the harm principle, which essentially states that people should be able to do whatever they want so long as they aren't harming anyone else. But harm is not always obvious"—Harold closed his eyes—"and what people do always affects other people." The narrator's voice quivered, as if managing rage.

A snippet of an unfamiliar voice giving a speech came on. "The United States was built on genocide and slavery. It has no sense of honor or duty; it is haunted—cursed. The United States values freedom—which, in the end, is indistinguishable from slavery . . ." Harold, in the heat, remembered the Shepherd College ad he'd seen on Instagram, and the image of the dean's secretary. He leaned back, but his arm involuntarily jolted, and he dropped his phone. His headphones unplugged and his phone landed on the floor, now playing the video through its speaker.

"In Ancient Greece," the video went on, "freedom always meant self-mastery."

"Oh," Mike said, reaching down.

"People wanted freedom to self-govern," the video continued, "but Americans want freedom *from,* not freedom *to.* Americans want freedom from history, from family, from everything that they don't consciously *choose.*" Mike moved as if in slow motion; the video seemed to play at double speed—Harold was embarrassed. "They are nihilists," the video said as Mike finally gripped Harold's phone, "but they are nihilists with no sense of their nihilism. Mishima was a nihilist in the great tradition of nihilism. Americans are vegetative nihilists, in a television stupor, waddling, drooling . . ."— Mike handed Harold the phone—"Timeless, placeless, peopleless . . . Nihilists who twist their necks and stick their heads in dark crevices . . ."—Harold's hand shook as he tried to tap the pause button on the screen and missed—"Nihilists afraid of their own nihilism . . ." Harold finally stopped the video.

The men in the sauna were quiet now as Harold fumbled with his phone and tried to act like nothing had happened. The chances that they would care or would have even been listening to the snippet that played from his phone seemed vanishingly small. Harold tried to reinsert his headphones, but they were uncomfortably hot now, and so Harold stood, wrapped his phone and headphones in the towel that had been draped around his shoulders, opened the sauna door a crack, and set the towel down onto the floor outside the sauna. Harold began to dizzily perceive his behavior as "suspicious," as if he'd moved his phone because he'd been exposed for what he was watching, and not because it had gotten extremely hot. As Harold closed the sauna door and re-approached where he'd been sitting, he noticed his butt sweat marks, which appeared black on the dark wood, and the pool of sweat beneath: he was pleased; he had been sweating and hadn't noticed. Nice.

Harold leaned back and closed his eyes. But as he closed them, the men in the sauna resumed their conversation, and their tone made Harold's eyes snap open again in horror.

"Mishima wanted to restore honor to Japan, and he wanted to have a supple form when he died," the Asian man said.

What the hell, Harold thought, alarmed. The heat hung low over him now.

"Kevin," the Asian man said, holding out his hand to Harold.

"Harold." Harold held out his hand.

He wondered if Casey was coming, if he might just show up out of nowhere, and what he'd have to say about all this. Did they happen to be talking about Mishima at the exact moment the video was talking about Mishima? Had Harold's phone somehow been simultaneously playing the video in his headphones and also through the speakers? No . . .

If Casey were here, this wouldn't have happened in the first place, Harold thought, because Harold wouldn't have been watching the video.

Harold tried to imagine himself as Casey; he tried to listen to the sauna conversation "as Casey"—to think like Casey would think—even going so far as to picture himself looking exactly like Casey, so that maybe he could find something to say.

"In the end," Kevin said, "all of history is leading toward the synthesis of the abstract and concrete, and a lifter gets a glimpse of it each time he is in the gym."

Harold glanced at Darrell's thigh. He imagined himself filming his new fitness YouTube channel.

Bodies communicate values, Harold thought-talked, imagining himself narrating his YouTube video. It is not right for a man to display his spiritual vice for all to see.

Mike and Darrell appeared many yards away from Harold now, as if they were shrinking, being pulled into a point in the distance.

"Mishima didn't compete in bodybuilding," Kevin said. Harold imagined that he was filming him. "He wanted to glorify his country. He wanted to restore spiritual order in his country. Actually, my country." He laughed. "He wanted to enter into the imagination . . . death . . ."

"You've got some good definition," Darrell said, grabbing Kevin's arm and inspecting it. "Not bad."

"Death," Kevin said, his voice thickly mixing with the heat, "permeates life. Death is primary; life is the aberration. Weightlifting uncovers many mysteries— but not death."

Harold glanced at the corner of the towel containing his phone through the clear pane in the sauna door. It had likely cooled off a little now. Maybe he could go retrieve it and film them covertly for his inaugural episode of English Lifterature . . .

"My imagination used to destroy me," Kevin said. "I would receive visions of total world destruction. I'd anticipate the end. I'd envision it constantly. I'd yearn for it. Now, because I'm stronger, I don't fear these things. Those frightful images of total annihilation have transformed into a profound sense of duty."

Harold felt like he was dreaming, or dreaming in a dream, where everything was at a distance from him.

Mike and Darrell were both shimmering. Their

skin dripped. Kevin's skin was wet, but he continually wiped himself off with a towel, then folded the towel and set it carefully down next to him.

"Death does not make everything absurd," Kevin said, "but it makes everything meaningful. Death is the meaning of life. Everything revolves around death."

The sauna felt uncomfortably hot now.

Harold thought of Shepherd.

"Death will come for all of us," Darrell said, in a clumsily affected tone, almost like he was trying to imitate Kevin. His voice sounded like watery blocks clunking down a set of stairs.

Shepherd, Harold thought dizzily. Harold wanted to speak but couldn't remember what he wanted to say. For a moment, his heartbeat picked up and his head felt light. Why couldn't he just be like Casey?

The sweat below looked even blacker now, as droplets from Harold's brow disappeared down into it.

Death ... or, lust ... Harold couldn't finish his thought. The brown heat permeated him, his chest swelling golden, brown eyes, silvery jutting voices.

The sauna made Harold's thoughts feel impossible.

He envisioned the people in the gym: silver eyes, pale gray skin. He saw them slowly decomposing.

Casey, he thought again, desperately. Once, he'd overheard Vance discussing Casey's "gym-going" with a visiting professor. The visiting professor, whose body resembled spaghetti sloping down the side of a wide bowl, said that people who worked out were working out *against death*, that they were ultimately trying to fight death, but they would die just the same as everyone else, so working out was a waste of time. "We're all going to die," the visiting professor had said, "and no amount of working out will change that. How is lifting even *useful*?"

It was obvious to everyone that all people died. This was not the profound realization that invertebrate shirkers liked to imagine it was. The truth, Harold knew, was that the dead were also among us. The dead inhabited dead flesh, and moved around.

It was inconceivable to the dead that there might be those who were living, and who, in a joyous display of life, engaged in vital activities, the sole sake of which was the propagation and enhancement of life. A defining characteristic of the dead, Harold thought, was their active hostility toward things that were not clearly useful. The dead cannot stand the living, and therefore want to cram everyone into a drawer labeled "useful" . . .

Mike shook his arms one at a time, muscles bouncing like raw meat, which then contracted into their normal, taut shape. Darrell wiggled his giant calves, then spoke again, but Harold had no idea what he was talking about. Was he singing? Kevin appeared amused.

"What were you watching?" Kevin said, directly addressing Harold now.

"I don't know," Harold said sheepishly. "I kind of just let the algorithm take me . . ."

The conversation made Harold feel tense, as if in anticipation of a blow. But the sauna relaxed him, and the endorphins from his workout were still giving him a mild euphoria.

"It sounded interesting," Mike said, glassy-eyed. "But if people here are—whatever, vegetables—it's because they want to be. For better or for worse, people in America are free. There has never been a country like America, a country based on ideas . . ."

When strong, attractive people spoke, no matter how inarticulately or contrary to his own opinions, Harold could usually see their point, and if he couldn't see their point, he wasn't bothered by it.

The market is bullshit, Harold thought-talked, imagining himself, again, narrating a video for his new YouTube channel, semi-imitating what he thought Yukio Mishima might say, and ignoring the conversation between the other three, blinking limply and occasionally nodding as if he were listening. Most people don't know what they want, Harold thought-talked. Their desires are mediated by others. The market encourages competition. But competition doesn't produce greatness—it produces homogeneity, and crap. We need the great to be exalted. Beauty, power, strength, honor . . . The market doesn't select for that.

What you are describing, Harold thought-talked, this time as an interlocutor, is fascism. Too strong a state always veers into evil and incompetence. If you leave people alone, they will get creative and figure it out. We want to organize society to maximize the productive expression of human creativity, which governments and bureaucracies crush. Fascism does not account for our creative potential. People are, on average, more capable and inventive than you give them credit for.

Human creativity is a spiral, Harold thought-talked,

countering his interlocutor, blocking out the voices in the sauna by closing his eyes. It travels downward. It needs to be directed up. Unless there is something strong pulling us up, Harold thought-talked, our creativity is always concerned with the depths. We are pulled inexorably down. We even use colloquialisms like "get to the bottom of things." Left to our own devices, we are depraved and wicked beasts, content only when everything is burning and destroyed. Of course, Harold thought-talked and looked at Mike, trying to act natural, as if he wasn't thought-talking and completely ignoring whatever they were talking about now, which seemed to have moved on from Harold's video, we have our reasons. But human reason is even worse than human creativity. Our creativity makes us destroy everything and our reason helps us explain it all afterward. We need order. Order—and strength, as well as beauty. We need something to look up at. This cannot be dictated by the market. The market is a spiral too. We need something other than what's merely *most popular*. And popularity is what the market gives you. That, and cronyism. The market is a leveler like any other leveler.

Mike and Darrell were laughing with Kevin now. They'd forgotten Harold just as quickly as they'd acknowledged him.

I can see you have a very grim view of humanity, Harold thought-talked, imagining now a debate on his lifting channel, but I think my view is more realistic. More holistic. Some human creativity is a spiral, but some ascends. You say people's creativity is a spiral.

Well, I think tyrannical control is a brick, and we use it to bludgeon and stifle what we can't control.

Harold interrupted himself, thought-talking as the other debater. The idea that people want what's best for themselves is completely unfounded. People want things that are bad for them all the time. People want what's bad for them, then get what's bad for them, then suffer—and then they blame other people and act out against them. We are blind, propelled by contradictory forces. Plus, if people want what's best for them, and they use control as a brick, isn't that just them exercising their so-called freedom? What mechanism is in place to stop them?

Let me fi— Harold thought-talked as Mike's slick, smooth tricep jiggled and he motioned with his arm toward Darrell. The heat was swirling inside him now. It was blossoming up into his eyes.

"I'm hungry," Darrell said, snapping Harold out of his thought-talk.

Harold was hungry too.

"Let's go," Darrell said.

Mike's sweat drummed against the floor like rain. He wiped his hand through his hair, flicking sweat back against the sauna wall behind him.

Darrell's mouth moved; it looked like he was chewing cud.

When Mike and Darrell stood, Kevin stood too, and the three of them nodded slightly at Harold; Darrell opened the door; Harold's skin felt briefly cooler, and he watched as their backs disappeared through the door.

VIII

<hr />

HAROLD WRAPPED HIS ARMS AROUND HIM-
self and forcibly breathed in loud spurts, like panting, or
trying to whisper a scream. He focused on making his
breaths slower and longer; he reached for the soap dis-
penser on the wall; he squirted a few lines into his hand.

The white tiled floor and the white tiled walls
seemed to glow, as freezing water shot down in
sheets. Harold shook his head. His chest opened up,
the whole of him opened up, and a kind of muted
joy burst through. His body absorbed the shock of
cold; his mind entered into it; his thoughts became
breath; then his thoughts turned to blood and coursed
through his body.

In the best moments, thoughts became blood. The
white walls opened too, until Harold was standing in
a vast expanse of white, or blue.

After he turned the shower off, he toweled off; the towel was small, and didn't absorb the water, so Harold basically pushed the water off his body with the towel like a squeegee. He wrapped the towel around his torso.

The white and green and even gray around him seemed more vivid, his mind swelling gold, as he dressed and grabbed the backpack, then left the locker room, dropping the white towels into a black hole, then entering the bright—though this time less sharp—gym, past the refrigerator and rows of protein snacks, past the front desk. Harold descended the stairs.

Harold's car felt like an extension of his body, arms still engorged, fused with the steering wheel; the rhythm of the car was the same as his breath, as if his heart beat into the engine, or the engine rumbled into him, and he thoughtlessly navigated around other machines in the sun.

THREE

I
=

WHEN ONE IS LIVING IN ANTICIPATION OF some negative event—whether rooted in an external threat or ambiguously bubbling up from within—he simultaneously expects it and does not expect it; it dimly hums at the base of his brain, but he is able to ignore it with tasks and other preoccupations. Often, this gnawing sense that something is lurking just around the corner—this waiting with certainty for some unforeseen bad thing to happen; negative faith— is just a part of oneself recognizing another part, but unwilling to fully acknowledge it. Things that seem external are within—they are just too frightening to look at directly.

Harold whistled as he drove home from the gym. He felt renewed. The roads through the hills snaked, then let out onto a straight stretch of road; the towering mountains caused a humbling shift in perspective; they shrunk Harold down, as if his concerns, in the absence of real mountains, rose to their size and became them, but in the presence of looming hills they cowered into insignificance. It was a blessing to be pumped and zooming through near-empty streets. Harold felt great.

Like pain, relief always felt new. Harold pulled off the main road into a nearby plaza and filled a cardboard container with items from the hot bar at the market: barbecue chicken, macaroni and cheese, steamed broccoli, sauteed kale; he bought coconut water. He ate alone in his car, looking at memes.

Then his phone started buzzing; the ringtone blasted through the speakers, interrupting Vivaldi. Harold didn't recognize the number. He pressed the button on the side of his phone. When the music came back on, he felt the sun. His face softened.

But the phone started ringing again. Ffff.

He picked up.

The voice on the other end, traversing time and space through invisible signals to Harold sitting there in his motionless car, seemed to billow out into him, entering his ear and gusting down into his gut; a hint of some familiar tone, some roundedness that Harold dimly recognized but couldn't place—all he knew was that it struck fear in his core.

Had he forgotten an appointment? Did someone die?

"Hey," Harold said, awkwardly feigning familiarity.

But as the voice spoke again, Harold's understanding caught up with him: it was Vance, asking if Harold was still on campus.

"No," Harold said, "but—"

Vance asked Harold if he would mind coming back, "just for a moment," to help "further discuss" some things that he and the department had "recently been made aware of."

Inside Harold something numbly welled. His brain sank into his neck. He put the car in gear, drove out of the parking lot and back onto the road, moving only according to the vague outline of cars, not paying attention to lights or any of the looming hills in his periphery, which appeared now as small bumps along the craterous face of the Earth.

II

THE HALLS AND DOORS APPEARED LIKE PULSING orbs, unnumbered silver shapes that drew Harold back now with an unusual pull as he walked on a narrow stone path cut into the grass, surrounded by thick beech trees and white oaks encircling small ponds, lined with large rocks, trying to envision the room he was meeting Vance in. Harold thought he saw something lying in the middle of the path up ahead—some sort of dog?—or goat?—he thought he could see horns—before getting closer and seeing it was just a fallen knotted tree branch . . .

Shepherd felt different, yet the same. The blood pumping through his muscles created a kind of inner motion that protected him from the usual stagnant, cyclical sensations the college usually instilled. Harold had parked a distance from Lawes, so he could walk a bit before the meeting. He liked to walk after meals, to aid digestion.

The spire of the Shepherd chapel shot up in the semi-distance; Harold followed it down until the church disappeared behind colonial brick; a gust of wind caused his lips to stretch open; he muscled them shut, but the watery wind between his lips and gums created pockets of air that then burst as he closed them. He stretched his top lip down even farther, noticing the skin beneath his nose, as a few new air bubbles emerged and then burst. He stretched his mouth out, like a smile, teeth exposed, trying to adjust back to a comfortable position as he approached the art library, its glass and silver awning glinting, somehow adding to the cold.

Harold shivered slightly. The deeper he got into campus, the more his calm turned into a foreboding, chilly fear.

Harold had spent so much time trying to ignore the reality that he could—and likely would—get in trouble, compartmentalizing the vague thrill he experienced so that it only lightly gnawed, manifesting occasionally as a burst of resentment, but for the most part absent from Harold's awareness; at times, he'd tried to go over all the possible ways he might get caught, but, finding them too numerous, and the potential punishments too unpredictable, he'd given up completely, resigning himself to the reality that if the department wanted to join forces against him, they'd be able to do what they willed. Such was the case with society, he thought—it always converged upon a single individual. This reality was evident daily, in snippets of conversations he'd overhear about faculty at other colleges, or authors whose books had been panned; he'd witnessed consensus formed in real time, among people he knew had held different opinions only moments prior; and he'd observed how this consensus was a weapon, used always by a group against an individual. Christianity was right about this, Harold knew: gossip was murder. People got together and conjured someone simply to kill them; Harold would fall victim to this, was undoubtedly already a victim of this, and would likely be the victim of something much worse very soon.

Casey had basically told him this would happen. Casey had no idea about the backpack, and certain other things, but the fact remained, Harold thought, all the same.

Pay attention to the tones, Casey told him. Words often had a shaded quality, like shadows, and each syllable combined to make a phrase that contained a hidden force within it, something those uttering them tried to hide, even to themselves. When Harold had received a recent email about there being something they could "use his help with," he'd felt plagued by preemptive guilt, despite his relative innocence. There was so much wrong with the college—why should they care about him? Yet he could feel it through the screen then, just as he felt it now: something was about to change.

Harold carried the backpack past the architecture building. He'd decided to bring it, in case that's what they wanted to talk to him about. It would seem too brazen, Harold reasoned, for him to bring *a stolen backpack* to the meeting with him. Especially to bring *a stolen backpack with a knife in it*—even if it was just a paper knife. If accused, he would simply feign ignorance, and say that it was his gym bag. It did, after all, have his gym clothes in it. *What kind of psycho would bring a stolen bag back to the scene of the crime?* he imagined saying, in a good-natured tone, the phrase "scene of the crime" accomplishing the double-motion of being slightly hyperbolic but also bringing the accusation out into the open: they'd be calling him a criminal. His hands were shaking from the cold.

The architecture building was newly rebuilt to resemble the original campus buildings, many of which had been torn down to make more "energy efficient" dwellings. But then a few of those were torn down yet again to make these new-old-style buildings, at the behest of a group of donors, who didn't like the way that Shepherd had come to resemble so little the college they remembered from their youth.

Harold spit on the grass. He effortfully resisted the architecture building's grim machinations, which seemed haunted by its own purpose—needlessly new, yet gesturing to something much older—like all things at Shepherd, creepily oscillating between the past and the future.

Lawes was fast approaching; Harold was walking with purpose now; he felt a surge of power; when he could clearly read the letters that spelled LAWES, he slowed to a stroll, so that he wouldn't be out of breath when he arrived. He wanted to be calm. He put his hands in his pockets to appear normal, then took one hand out, so as not to seem suspiciously normal... However, feeling unbearably awkward at the imbalance, he put his loose hand back in his pocket and continued at an unhurried pace.

Either way, it would be fine, he thought, bracing himself. If they fired him, he wouldn't fight. He could always just go work at a gym... He wondered if the Hill's employees would welcome him... The fitness industry was so overpopulated, and he was not uniquely qualified for it in any way... His lifting channel...

Harold was uniquely qualified to teach literature. He loved literature, and he wanted to model that love for his students. His acidic fluid hawking was really just a complicated love; he felt so differently about his job after a lift; everything felt less zombified; there was still hope that an individual, through love, could make a difference in one or two students, simply through modeling this love—any student with a spark would recognize it shining among the muted hues.

The brown-red of Lawes appeared almost black as it took shape. Behind it, in the far distance, was a dirt-red rock face. Harold would take what came; he wouldn't let them gang up on him. Lifting had taught him everything he needed to know—now it was time for action.

III

HAROLD WALKED PAST THE MEETING ROOM door and into the bathroom around the corner. What was he doing? It was completely stupid to bring the backpack to the meeting. What if the student had given a description of the bag? They would recognize it instantly. Plus, there was a weapon in it. He should have just declined to come in, or thrown the backpack away and denied everything. It would have been easy. It would have been the easiest thing in the world. But this is the world we live in now, Harold reminded himself, everything is upside down.

Harold shoved the backpack into the trash. He wet a bunch of paper towels and scattered them over the backpack, pushing the backpack deeper into the trash as he did.

He felt a faint regret as his body straightened up—his heart swelled as he thought of the paper knife—he could always come back and grab it after the meeting if he wanted to.

In the mirror, the edges of his eyes appeared softer. He practiced making faces. He felt prepared now for whatever came. Vance, David, John—it didn't matter. Harold would vanquish them. They were nothing. They were less than nothing. He was ready.

But what about the cameras? Were there cameras outside the bathroom?

No—Harold had gotten away with it. Even if they came into the bathroom, and exhumed the backpack, and even if they had Harold on video entering the bathroom with the backpack and leaving without it—as well as the testimony of the students who had barged in and seen him with it—Harold could still deny it all. And if he denied it firmly and convincingly—if he believed it himself—it would become true. There was nothing they could do to him. He was free. He was free!

Harold washed his hands and padded the trash with more paper towels as he dried them. When he exited the bathroom, and arrived at the door through which his fate would be decided, he paused and flexed his glutes. He flexed his pecs—his muscles felt full.

IV

THE DARK WOOD BOOKSHELF CONTRASTED with the light gray desk where the administrators sat, behind which Dolly and Vance stood, filling Harold, inexplicably, with something like lust. There was a novelty to his surroundings that enticed him. My life could still change, Harold thought. There are still new places, with new people in them; I could become somebody new.

One of the administrators offered Harold a bottle of water, which he declined; but then, seeing the other administrator take a sip, he changed his mind and accepted.

Harold reached out to receive the water, thanking the woman as his fingers unfurled, then curled around it. He opened the crinkling bottle and sipped.

"Vance said you're coming from the gym?" the

female administrator said. She had black hair and mole-like features. She introduced herself and the other administrator. "I hope we didn't cut your work-out short."

"I'm coming from the gym," Harold said, matching her tone. Her long, manicured nails tapped the plastic of her water bottle. Harold wanted to address her by name but had already forgotten it.

"I was actually just leaving when Vance called," he said. "I had to pass the school anyway," he lied. "It worked out perfectly."

The male administrator made a noise. "I know I'd hate it if one of these stupid things made me cut a lift short."

This tone of camaraderie surprised Harold, who quickly gauged his physique. Though he wore a col-lared shirt and a jacket, Harold could discern that the man had broad shoulders, with a well-developed chest: the top button of his shirt was undone; his neck pressed up against the fabric.

The female administrator thanked Harold for be-ing there. Dolly had just been telling her about their "brutal" meeting earlier, she said, and so she appre-ciated Harold's willingness to come back to campus. "I know you must be drained," she said, locking eyes with Harold. She tilted her head toward Dolly. Harold felt warm. Dolly smiled.

"Brutal," Dolly echoed, no trace of her accent. She swiveled her head on her neck. "Hooey," she said, ac-cented now, though her tone still retained some of the strain of when she'd echoed the administrator's.

The cool air from outside still lingered on Harold's skin, but inside he remained warm, in part due to his blood, which was still pumping into his muscles, such that the dissonance between the internal and external was vast and impenetrable: his flesh was tight against his frame, shrunken from cold; but inside, he was warmly engorged.

Were they laying some sort of trap? Harold knew that it would be risky to say too much specifically. Everything was a kind of dance . . . They were dancing . . . Harold had presumed he was alone in his meeting-disdain—alone with Casey, rather (who, though absent, remained a kind of presence there in Harold's mind)—and it would take some kind of dark miracle to convince him otherwise. Harold had been there, after all. He had seen the nodding, bobbling heads.

The female administrator and Dolly certainly seemed to be hinting at a shared understanding . . . But then again . . .

"Brutal," Harold said.

After so much uncertainty, the time had finally come. For a moment, Harold felt worried that he wouldn't be able to hear anyone; a bloody silence filled his ears. Are my ears filled with blood? he thought. What have I done?

Harold tried not to bite his lips or stamp his feet . . . He bit his lips . . .

"Tell us a bit about your relationship with Casey," the female administrator said.

Harold felt like he was underwater. "I, we—we lift together sometimes, why?"

Was Harold going to get fired? He felt a sudden rage; everything was real; he did not want to work here anymore—he wanted to kill them—*I hate them—I hate them!*

The backpack . . .

"We've received some reports," the female administrator said as the soggy room swirled, "from people who wish to remain anonymous, that Casey has been teaching certain texts, saying things during lectures that have been causing harm in our community."

Harold flexed his pecs—nice and tight. What did Casey have to do with this? Casey hadn't mentioned anything. Everybody loved Casey. Where was he now?

Harold quietly shuffled his feet.

When Harold asked them why they were asking about Casey, his tone was defensive. The faces appeared dumbfounded. Harold looked into the corner of the room, so he couldn't discern their expressions exactly, but he could feel the dumbfoundedness, a room full of dumbfoundedness . . .

"Why don't you talk to Casey?" he asked. He was having trouble modulating his tone, and in his attempt not to raise his voice he had accidentally sounded like a hurt dog.

There was a slight pause. Did they not hear him? *On with it*, he wanted to yell, *come on with it!* He started moving the air in his throat, getting ready to speak, when the female administrator informed him that they had, in fact, spoken to Casey.

So maybe this was why he hadn't shown up to the

meeting, or the gym? But what had happened? Harold wanted to get up and run back to the bathroom, grab the backpack.

The female administrator shifted. "We have to go through a whole process," she said, "when we receive these kinds of complaints. It can feel a little arduous, but we need to be as thorough as possible. That way it's not just Casey against whoever made the complaint. With more people, it's more fair. More *democratic*. We can get a fuller picture."

Harold watched in half terror as the administrator moved his arms up from his lap to the table. His arms were girthy, yet tight. A vision of Harold's own hands flashed before him, like a phantom, and, though he could have simply looked down at his hands, he chose to imagine them instead: withered, thin—pale in comparison.

The eyes in the room felt like scalpels; he couldn't think because of all the eyes; he turned his neck and scanned them, all eight of them, a sort of blur, but when he focused his own, he noticed that some weren't looking at him—they were looking down or past him or at each other.

"Why are we here?" he asked, more timidly than intended.

"We can't provide exact details," the female administrator said, shuffling papers. Her tone had taken on an icy quality, like there was a threat beneath it. But there was also a subtle, clearly intended friendliness, like she was comforting him in the wake of some loss. "Since the investigation is ongoing, we just wanted to get a better sense of what might be going on, to see if there might be a pattern . . ."

The blurrier things became, and the more time that elapsed without clarification, the more panicked Harold felt. He felt as if everything within him was moving a hundred miles an hour, but he could not move his limbs, like a night terror. A stabbing vagueness gripped him, somehow stuck itself deep in his core.

The chair, however, was significantly more comfortable than the chair he'd sat on before, and, though he was essentially paralyzed, his body still felt good, buzzing with endorphins from the workout. He sunk deeper, as if into a cloud; he wanted to kill everyone in the room; the walls groaned, but this time at a higher pitch; at once, Harold remembered tenure, his desire for tenure; he wanted to threaten Vance, Dolly, David; *Harold* deserved tenure; he was sick of slaving away, dealing with atrocities like this.

The female administrator adjusted her glasses.

He touched his right ear in the place where his glasses would have rested if he wore them.

The energy in the back of his head shot to the front of his face, rushing in. "I mean," he said, "I've never been with Casey in the classroom . . ."

Until then, Vance and Dolly had seemed like cardboard cutouts of themselves. Now Dolly came to life.

"Well," she said, before lapsing back into stillness.

There are times when people hide things from each other, and times when people hide things from themselves, and although he felt, due to the nature of the meeting, that he was in the former situation, he couldn't help but suspect that he was also in the latter: he didn't know what Dolly was asking for, but a deep part of him had begun to separate itself from his conscious thought, like meat from a bone.

The sensation was twofold. On one level, he could hear that his tone was confrontational, and he wanted to hurt them; but on another, he felt a calm relief seeping through his damp rage. He had hated them for so long; his hatred had finally reached a screeching pitch; but potential reconciliation set itself down in his bones, beneath his muscle, like something shorn up from the ancient past, deep inside him, deeper than him, growing alongside his blind rage toward his colleagues, the administrators, Shepherd College itself.

The administrators asked about Casey: what kinds of things Harold and Casey talked about; what Casey believed as it pertained to pedagogy; whether or not Harold had ever heard him say anything that might, in another context, make students uncomfortable. It became clearer and clearer, with each new question— as Harold's astonishment grew in proportion to this clarity—that the meeting was not about Harold at all, but about Casey.

This added a new layer to his experience: though Harold felt defensive on behalf of Casey, he now wanted to make sure that the focus stayed on Casey, and away from Harold and the backpack. Were they deceiving him? Lulling him into a feeling of safety, until he let his guard down or accidentally said the wrong thing?

The male administrator unbuttoned the top button of his shirt with his meaty hands. He was stronger than Harold. His hair was cut primly, and his clothes were sharp and modern, but he had an air about him that made him appear ambiguously old, as if his clothing was masking the fact that he was as old as the university itself.

Harold clamped down, focused, trying to keep everything moving toward Casey alone.

The administrators' questions remained appropriately vague, such that he was never entirely certain what he was being asked; however, the more he spoke, the more he loosened up, and, gradually, he started answering amicably, so as not to inflame their curiosity. He wanted to clear himself of any negative affiliation with Casey, although he didn't even know what he was afraid that they'd find out. He didn't have anything to hide. Aside from the backpack... Harold wanted to go on vacation, to sit on the beach and read a novel...

Harold tried to appear reasonable and willing to comply, and as he focused more on responding to the administrators, instead of acting on abstract ideals, he began to notice that his animosity toward them faded, replaced by unexpected resentment toward Casey. Why hadn't he told Harold anything was going on? They were all gathered there because of Casey. And Harold and Casey were friends. Why had Casey let Harold get blindsided like this?

The administrators shifted in their seats. Vance and Dolly both watched them.

Harold's feelings were intense and hard to locate.

There was nothing, in theory, preventing him from just getting up and leaving, but paradoxically, the more questions the administrators asked—and the more Harold avoided their eyes to look at Dolly or Vance, who were themselves looking at the administrators—the more he felt pulled into the meeting. Instead of simply getting up and leaving, or lying out on the beach with a novel, what he actually wanted was to get pulled even closer, to enter into them and merge.

Harold had the bizarre sensation, which he dismissed instantly, that he wanted to *become* the administrators, to *become* Dolly and Vance. The sides of his face were creased, especially around the eyes, which were tired from being held in a fixed position. Harold's stomach and ears felt warm. Kill, he thought, with no direction. He felt enveloped in something warmer than the sauna now. Something that seemed to be coming from within; something like love.

For a minute or two, the administrators talked among themselves, with Dolly and Vance interjecting once or twice; Harold descended into his thoughts, trying to focus but feeling increasingly disturbed by Casey's absence in the sauna. Harold remembered their last interaction . . . how something had glinted in Casey's eye . . .

It felt almost mythological as Harold tried to remember what he thought about it then, having seen Casey's eye flash pure red, only for a moment before reverting to its normal blue. This, it seemed, was the key to understanding everything. Everything that had been transpiring in him, in the college, all the murderousness surrounding him and now within him, the backpack, all the classrooms like empty tombs, even his own theft—everything reflected in Casey's eye, flashing red.

Harold's skin felt clammy—he already missed the gym—he was hungry again; he briefly imagined what he might eat at home: chicken and rice, a frozen pizza; he was trying to remember if he had sandwich ingredients in the refrigerator when a thought he'd never had before came over him, like light: he hated Casey.

As every academic knew, it was rare to have any truly new thoughts: most thoughts were just variations of the same few thoughts, which came upon a person in their youth and then possessed them into adulthood, and so this new thought nearly caused Harold to choke; he hiccupped; he thought that he was coughing, sputtering and gasping, when in reality—he'd discerned in the same moment—he was sitting completely still with his new thought: he hated Casey. The hatred he had felt before had been misplaced: it was Casey whose eyes had betrayed him; it was Casey who'd given Harold advice, and who tried to tell Harold tenure was meaningless. What if Casey was secretly sabotaging him? Casey had "taught" Harold more than anyone at Shepherd. And Casey was the occasion for this meeting.

After a bit more back-and-forth, the meaning of which Harold was only distantly aware of, preoccupied as he was with his new thought, the administrators asked Harold to leave. They were going to discuss among themselves and call him back in momentarily.

"No," Harold said. "I can't explain it. But I can't leave."

The administrators seemed taken aback, then put at ease. Dolly's eyes appeared pure white, then glowed softly like amber. The administrators described in more detail what they needed. Some of what he'd said had been useful, but they needed Harold to write it all down for their records.

And so with Vance, Dolly, and the two administrators looking on, he wrote.

He started slowly, equivocating and trying to compliment Casey as best he could. Despite his newfound hatred, he still felt the need to preserve his sense of self as someone who was definitively "not a narc." Harold oscillated between not wanting to get Casey in trouble and wanting to give the administrators what they were looking for. He related a few off-color remarks Casey had made in private. There was the time he said that "European novels were the best," or the time he told Harold that a certain critic was "low IQ." He may have been joking, Harold wrote; a lot of the time Harold couldn't even tell whether he himself was joking about something, he confessed . . . Casey was a good guy, he wrote, but he knew it was not enough to be a "good guy" . . . It was important that they, as a department, set limits on what was acceptable, so that true freedom for everyone was possible, especially in light of recent events . . . Plus, Casey had requested documentation for anyone spending department funds . . . The day after he had spoken harshly with Dianthe . . . And the tone with which Casey had suggested it seemed to indicate a certain bias ... The pen seemed to move on its own, without Harold, as he remembered some complaints others had had about Casey over the years, and Harold parroted them on the page; he wrote against his will, or so in line with his will that he could do it unthinkingly; things began to crystalize; Harold just hadn't known ... all arrows pointed toward Casey ... he continued writing.

Casey had been a corrupting influence not just on Harold but on everyone ... He had convinced everyone that he was worthy of their esteem, when in reality he was worthy only of their contempt. Casey had said he wanted to ban "every discipline with 'studies' in the name," and that he "loved Knut Hamsun," and had all along been driving Harold to this meeting ... This was why everyone loved him—he had tricked them. It was all Casey's fault. Casey had darkened Harold's vision. It was Casey's fault entirely.

The eyes peering down at him burned holes into the back of Harold's head as he looked down at the paper; his body felt warm; his hand wasn't his hand; there were shouts outside the door; Harold snapped out of his trance for a moment, before becoming possessed by something profound and all-encompassing ...

HAROLD FELT LIKE he was coming down with a cold; his skin felt simultaneously cool and hot; he handed over his paper and sniffled. He flexed his right pec a few times, making it bounce beneath his button-up; it already felt a little flat ... He shook hands with everybody in the room except Dolly, who opted instead to wave at first, standing a mere few feet away—then suddenly came in for a hug.

The glass doors seemed to swing wider when he left than when he'd entered. It was as though someone had replaced them during the meeting. Harold walked through the familiar halls with new feet. He encountered the same scattered benches, plastic meant to look like wood beneath the bright fluorescent light, but now the benches gently organized themselves. He felt no violence bearing down on him; he heard no screaming walls. He navigated through the winding halls, which didn't jut now so much as form an intricate web of pleasingly varied passages . . .

A calm permeated Harold that couldn't be totally attributed to lifting.

The glimmering gray felt cool. All the scattered fragments became one.

What had he done?

A group of students walked past, some of whom he recognized, and Harold greeted them one by one. Harold ascended the stairs and noted a curious sensation of flight, like he was floating, like he'd been unknowingly carrying a heavy object that was mysteriously removed; the rubbed edges of the stairs felt like springboards; Harold was soaring.

He walked through the foyer toward the exit near the parking lot, then remembered that he'd parked in the lot a little farther off. He turned back to walk through Lawes, to exit through another door.

As Harold turned, he ran straight into David. His

heart rate increased, then quickly slowed to normal. David's gangly limbs did not molest him; nor did his head swell up and bobble. Everything was fine. They were even walking together, which seemed strange: when Harold bumped into David, he had been walking toward him, but now they were walking in the same direction. Harold did not spiral or have any secret seething thoughts. They discussed a new novel by a young female filmmaker, whom the college was considering hiring, about despair and a religious conversion, while walking in lockstep with one another, as Harold told David how he felt strangely reborn. He couldn't really explain it, and—perhaps sincerely, or perhaps just out of politeness—David said he felt something too. Their legs moved in unison, but whereas before this would have bothered Harold, causing him dayslong shame and embarrassment, their synchronized strolling did not make him want to strangle David, nor maul him with his fists, nor gauge his eyes out, nor kill himself. Rather, their unity seemed a curious coincidence, something that endeared Harold to David. Even if they disagreed about some minor things, there was nothing so severe to justify such animosity toward him. Harold listened now with extraordinary patience; he almost reached out to hold David's hand. Harold felt grateful.

As they walked outside in the brisk cold toward the parking lot, standing near a black, overflowing trash can, something otherworldly occurred: David asked if Harold would teach him how to deadlift. He had been doing kettlebell swings and Turkish get-ups, he said, but he was ready to "take it to the next level." The phrase caused no disturbance in Harold; he exhaled and felt free; in fact, he mirrored David's language when he told him that of course, he'd love to help him "take it to the next level," and that "it would be my honor," before making a jokey show of muscled confidence, doing a lat spread pose—fists on hips, chest and back puffed up and out.

V
##

THE NEXT MORNING, CASEY WASN'T IN HIS office. Harold thought to text him, but when he reached down for his phone, Dolly walked by. Her hair looked nice.

Maybe she had crimped it, or was wearing it in a new way? He looked down the hall, where each head now seemed distinct, and he clearly made out her head among them.

Standing in the narrow corridor near a cluster of offices, Harold turned back toward Casey's door. He imagined opening it and encountering Mel there instead of Casey.

Earlier, Harold had heard some hushed tones. He thought he'd heard Casey's name, but he dismissed it as his own imagination. But now, looking for Casey in his office, Harold was certain that they'd been talking about him.

It wasn't like Casey to be such a bad friend or employee. Lately he just hadn't been showing up for people. Harold remembered one of their recent lifts, when Casey grinded out a bench press PR as Harold stood above him. Casey had always been an inspiration. And Harold was grateful for his presence in the department and the gym. He wasn't a bad friend; he was one of Harold's best friends . . .

But the effect of his absence was undeniable, and Harold was grateful for this too. Harold went downstairs and taught, and even the students seemed to radiate a new kind of life. Their normal disinterested resistance struck Harold as zen-like, as opposed to obstinate, and he accepted their disengagement as he carried on without a care. He even laughed a couple of times, overcome with the sensation of being tickled. Life was not a book but a symphony; all one had to do was relax and enjoy it.

After class, Harold passed by Casey's office again. This time, his stuff was gone. Harold thought again of texting him. But what if he knew about what Harold had written? Or what if he didn't suspect him at all, and would be tipped off by Harold's overeager badgering? Had there been some kind of suspension? Or perhaps Casey had chosen to leave out of spite? Best not to annoy him now anyway, Harold thought. No need to make it all about himself.

The administrators, whose names Harold now

remembered, had assured him that everything would remain confidential—but who could trust these spineless bureaucrats? At Shepherd, you could not trust any of these . . . Harold abandoned the thought, which felt spiritless even as he thought it; a zombie-thought; polluted air wearing the husk of former thoughts, trying to haunt him . . .

Serenity permeated the halls, undeniable as it had been fraught with murderous tension a mere twenty-four hours ago. Nothing had changed, but somehow everything had changed.

Though Harold had no way of knowing about his conduct in the classroom, Casey was, now that he thought of it, the one who had turned him against his colleagues. Casey was the one who had taught him how to lift. Harold was always in conflict with his colleagues—what if this was because of Casey? Casey had influenced him against his colleagues, despite Casey's own good standing among them—but now the entire school was filled with light. The faces all appeared distinct. Perhaps there was no "crowd"—perhaps there was only Casey after all.

Sitting in his office, grading a paper that had piqued his interest, about J. K. Huysmans's *The Damned*, he considered that he would in fact miss Casey, if indeed he were actually gone, and not just on some suspension or temporary leave. Despite everything, Casey was highly intelligent, profoundly caring, and wise.

It occurred to Harold that Casey might not have been fired or suspended at all, but perhaps, learning of the pain he'd caused, he'd nobly chosen to absent himself, or resign, so as not to make any more students or colleagues uncomfortable. If he had known about the position he'd put Harold in, for example, perhaps he'd simply left on his behalf. Harold began to wonder if Casey was not, in the end, a kind of savior, having sacrificed himself for all their benefits, or for Harold's benefit specifically. Harold could not have predicted the kind of contentedness that now filled Lawes. It filled him, too. A kind of violent poetry possessed him. He wanted to jump and kick the air; he felt grateful to Casey for his new freedom; he wondered when or if he would see Casey in the gym again. But Casey felt already gone, like a memory.

Aha! Harold could text him, asking if he wanted to go to the gym; he didn't need to bring up anything suspicious about the meeting, or his absence. Harold texted him, trying to inhabit a past, out-of-reach nonchalance, but the text returned an automated message saying the number he tried to text was no longer in service.

Harold had no inkling then that this could be a bad omen, and felt only a gratitude. The inarticulate suspicion that Casey had been the cause of all Harold's problems at the college still seemed true, but the intuition had lost its hard edges; he could not remember with any specificity what those problems even were. Casey had been the cause of his disease, and now his absence was the cure. This was the only logical conclusion.

Now, without Casey, Harold would exist among his colleagues, maybe even thrive. There would be no

Casey holding him down. New possibilities sprouted like plants.

He sat at his desk, looking at his laptop, when there was a knock on his half-open door.

Dolly stood smiling, hand on the knob.

She made a joke about how "hard-oh" he appeared to be working, then asked if he had read a novel that had recently come out, which Harold had in fact read and enjoyed. Dolly said that she'd enjoyed it too.

David passed and, seeing Dolly in the doorway, slowed to a halt. The sun shone through the small office window as David and Dolly invited Harold to dinner before the upcoming colloquium.

Harold was acting in contradiction to almost everything he'd felt and thought since arriving at Shepherd, but he didn't feel contradicted; the awareness of his contradiction didn't enter his mind at all.

In fact, he felt stronger than ever.

ACKNOWLEDGMENTS

Thank you to Nicolette Polek, Michael Clune, Tao Lin, Kendall Storey, Chris Clemans, Scott McClanahan, Juliet Escoria, Patrick Reid, Red Nini Mode, Literary Drama, Ape-men 2, and my family.

JORDAN CASTRO is the author of *The Novelist* and two books of poems. His fiction and nonfiction have been published in *Harper's Magazine*, *The Point*, *Tin House*, *Muumuu House*, and elsewhere. He is the deputy director of the Cluny Institute and serves on the board of the Giancarlo DiTrapano Foundation for Literature and the Arts.